The Case Files of Owan Craig
Volume 1
H. A. Titus

The Case Files of Owan Craig: Volume 1 by H. A. Titus
Published by Fayette Press
www.fayettepress.com

Cover Designer: Magpie Designs

Printed in the United States of America

To my Contrarian ladies. Love you, even when you do try to embarrass the heck out of me. <3

THE LAST WORD

By the way all the stories start, you'd think it was always rainin' in New York City just before the hero gets dragged into a mess of trouble by a pretty girl.

But I swear, it really was rainin' that evening when I stepped into the Howler, a club just far enough off Main Street to not be *the* spot, but close enough that the hoity-toities didn't mind drinking there. Most of the folk there couldn't understand how the Howler kept itself from gettin' raided, given the Prohibition and all. I knew.

Giselle, the owner, was fae.

She stood behind the bar at the right side of the room, resplendent in a tight red dress that clung in all the right spots without looking trashy. Her hair was cut in a daring bob, and her heels made her taller than the rest of the women in the room. The top of her honey-blonde head was almost level with mine, and I was no slouch.

She looked up and made eye contact with me, and I immediately felt the glamour swirling around her. Fae glamour kept normal folks from seeing the bar as it really was. At the same time, it pulled them in with a powerful urge, making the Howler one of the most popular speakeasies around. Being half-fae myself, I could see through the glamour and resist its pull, but I figured since Giselle obviously wanted to talk to me, I should probably oblige her. After all, she gave me free drinks in return for the occasional pro bono job. I walked over to the bar and shucked my coat and hat, tossing them on the seat next to me.

"Evenin', Giselle."

One side of her lips curved up into a flirty smile. "Owan. The usual?"

I nodded carefully. So far, she seemed to be in a good mood, but I'd been around long enough to know that could change on a dime.

She set a glass down in front of me and poured in a measure of Irish honey whiskey. The rich amber color reflected off the polished surface of the bar as I picked up the glass and took a sip.

Giselle leaned her elbows on the bar, watching the door over my shoulder. Though ever the gracious hostess, there was a nervous energy in the way her glamour swirled through the air, sparkling off the low-lit lamps and candles on the tables. She caught me watching and ran her fingers through her hair, sweeping golden strands behind her pointed ears.

"So what did you need me for?" I asked.

She raised one elegant eyebrow. "What makes you think I need you, shamus?"

The term for private detective made me grin—Giselle rarely used slang.

"I dunno. It's just that every time you're in need of a little off-the-record help, my feet turn here of their own accord. D'ya know that tonight, I'd actually planned to go home and read? Rex Stout's new book came out last week, and I've had a copy sittin' in my flat for two days. Haven't even cracked the cover."

"Hmm. Sorry, baby." Her smile widened.

I kept grinning, even though my stomach turned. I'd been trying for five years, ever since I first met Giselle, to figure out how she'd laid a charm on me that set my feet to doin' whatever she asked. It went beyond the normal requirement of owing a favor—I was pretty sure I'd paid that debt to her long ago.

It wasn't in the way she prepared the drink, 'cause I'd watched her close, and she put no glamour into that whiskey. It wasn't when she touched me, 'cause I'd've felt it right away—instead, it had taken me near to six months of these "spontaneous" visits and the coincidences pilin' up before I realized the problem.

Folks didn't call Giselle a sly vixen for nothin'.

I downed the rest of the whiskey. No use in delaying the inevitable. "Whatcha need this time, doll?"

Lugh's Spear, she hated when I called her that. I could see the thunder clouds gathering in her pretty whiskey-colored eyes, turning them a burnt-sugar brown. Then she blinked, and the smile and the twinkle in her eyes was back in full force.

"There's a new hire. Roe Gillam." Giselle reached out, traced a circle on the back of my hand. "She's having a bit of an issue with a patron."

Her touch was cold as ice. I forced myself still, though the tickle of her fingers sent chills up my back and made the hair on my arms rise. My eyes focused on her lips, her soft smile. She was *gorgeous* tonight. Things around me faded to a fuzzy gold, and I leaned forward slightly.

Outside, thunder crackled, and I jumped. The movement jarred Giselle's hand off my arm, and the glamour snapped. My heartbeat sped up. She'd almost had me there. I met her gaze, took a deep breath.

"So what d'ya want from me?" I asked, keeping my eyes locked on hers.

"Just a little lesson. Nothing much," she purred. "But enough that he'll leave the girl alone."

"You can't block him from entering?" I checked the red-and-gold-shaded lamp hanging beside the door. It was one of the stronger anchor points for her glamour wards. A thick flurry of glamour floated around it, meaning the wards were in good working order.

She pouted. "No."

I raised an eyebrow. *Saints*. "You can't just change Roe's work schedule?"

"He always seems to know."

I swore and wished I hadn't already finished the whiskey. "I dunno, Giselle ..."

Her red lips pushed outward in a pout, and she traced another circle on the back of my hand. This time, I could feel the slight nudge of power she put into it. I raised a second skin of my own glamour along my arm.

Again, the thunderstorm in her eyes flared, along with a crack of more thunder outside. "Come, now, Owan. This guy's done nothing too forward yet, but Roe's scared. She doesn't even like to walk home by herself anymore."

"Appealin' to my chivalry is a low blow, Giselle."

Another grin. "So you'll do it?"

I sighed. "Aye. Where's the girl?"

Giselle nodded at a point in space somewhere over my

left shoulder. I spun to my right, swinging the barstool all the way around so I could lean my elbows on the bar. No use in askin' for bad luck by going around widdershins.

A jazz quartet was setting up at the other side of the room on the small central stage, while another guy in a newsie's cap was sweeping and polishing the dance floor. It was near seven o'clock, and most speakeasies would be bouncing by now, but the Howler served fae and those who dealt with them. Things really got movin' here closer to what normals would consider breakfast time the next morning.

Some of Giselle's girls were weaving among the tables, serving the few customers that had already showed up. Giselle only employed women as waitresses, but she treated them well, and usually had no issue with kicking out wise guys who tried to get too handsy. The fact that she wanted me to take care of this guy for her made me uneasy.

"Which one's Roe?" I asked.

"The redhead."

Redhead was a bit of an understatement—Roe's hair was gloriously bright and curly, with the kind of soft shimmer that made a man want to run his fingers through it. She wore it swept up and secured with pins and a sequined headband. Even halfway across the room I could see the freckles dotting her nose and cheeks, adding a touch of warmth to her pale skin.

"Pretty, isn't she?" Giselle asked.

I picked up my drink, trying to figure how best to answer.

"Baby," she whispered, lips tickling my ear. "You forget, I can feel it when your heartbeat speeds up."

I eased my arm away from her grip and kept watching Roe.

Despite the wide grin on her face, she seemed skittish. Her blue eyes darted about the room, bright and birdlike, even as she chatted with customers.

So the problem guy wasn't here yet, else she'd be looking at one spot a lot more. I turned back to Giselle, keeping my eyes fixed on the big mirror behind the bar. I could just see Roe in it.

If Giselle couldn't ban the guy, that meant one of two things: she was afraid of him, or he was more powerful than any glamoured wards she could muster.

I couldn't see Giselle being scared of anyone. Wary, maybe. She should've been able to keep this guy out, if she wanted. But she obviously didn't, and so she'd called on her pet watchdog.

I growled under my breath.

Giselle's lips curved up in an impish smile. "Excuse me, baby, but I've got to go greet a few people."

Giselle moved away and motioned to Roe to come take her place behind the bar. As Roe passed me, she smiled, a warm and open smile that spoke of genuine friendship as opposed to Giselle's flirtatiousness. "Evening," she said, in a slight drawl of a Midwestern accent. Not a native, then.

"Evenin'," I replied.

Behind us, the band started to play a jazzy ragtime number. Roe turned and pulled a couple of bottles down from the mirrored shelving behind the bar.

The bell over the door rang. I deliberately didn't move, but Roe straightened, and her lips parted as she sucked in a sharp hiss.

"Roe! Baby doll. Let's see a sidecar, would ya?" The voice was loud and brash. Its owner moved into my peripheral vision—a tall, slim guy with dark hair parted to the side. He wore a nice suit, gray with darker gray pinstripes. He dropped his hat on the bar and straddled a bar stool. As he leaned his elbows on the bar, I could see the outline of a knife press into his jacket. His ears were just this side of fae—not fully pointed, but not rounded like a full human's. Half-fae, like me.

Roe set a glass down in front of the man with a sharp clink. Liquor sloshed over the side, dripping to the bar. "Why are you here again?" she demanded.

He leered, brushing his thumb along her knuckles as he

moved the glass closer to himself. Roe started to move away, but—quick as a wink—the guy's hand snaked out and pinned her wrist to the bar. His chuckle sounded like grinding gravel.

I clenched my hand under the bar.

Roe put her free hand on the guy's arm and dug her painted, sharp nails into him. He winced, and his expression shifted from a mocking smile to thinned lips, eyes fixed on Roe.

"That hurts, doll."

"Giselle and I've both warned you, Eric," she whispered.

He laughed derisively. "Your boss don't care, Roe, otherwise she would've banned me. 'Fraid you're on your own here."

Roe gritted her teeth.

Eric stood, brought his right hand up to her face, and brushed a curl away from her ear. She tried to jerk away, but his fingers went around the back of her neck. He pulled her forward, lips almost touching hers, and whispered, "Roe. C'mon, kitten. What're you afraid of?"

"Not you," Roe snapped, the quickness to her words belying the faint tremble in her voice.

He laughed again.

I didn't like that laugh. It had a nasty tone. And I didn't like the dark look in his eyes. Dammit, Giselle knew me too well. I couldn't let this continue.

"All right, I figure that's about enough," I said, swinging around to face Eric.

Eric glanced at me out of the corner of his eyes, then looked back at Roe. "Why don't you fade, pal. This don't concern you."

"You're speaking loudly enough that it could be the entire place's concern," I said.

"Go get a white ten-gallon hat, bruno."

I looked at Roe. "He botherin' you?"

"Very much so," she replied between gritted teeth.

"You heard the lady. I think it's time for *you* to fade."

Eric released Roe and turned to fully face me. "Tryin' to be smart? Listen, it's just a spat between me and my dame here, no reason to get worked up."

Giselle came up beside Roe and put her hand on the bar between us. "Gentlemen. If you're going to continue this discussion, might I suggest you take it outside? You're beginning to disturb my other customers."

I tried not to wince. With how fast she'd gotten between us, any fool would be able to see that she'd been waitin' for something to happen.

Eric looked between Giselle and me, and his face

hardened. "I see how it is. Can't even stand up to me yourself, huh, Giselle? Gotta have one of your boys do it." He snorted and snatched his hat from the bar, then headed for the door.

Well, so much for makin' it look like Giselle ain't involved.

Giselle darted a half-panicked look at me. "Go after him!"

"Why?" I said. "He's gone, ain't that what you wanted?"

Giselle gave me a meaningful look, and before I realized what was happening, my feet were carrying me after Eric. I stopped and braced myself, expecting to feel a painful tugging at my heart, a rolling in my gut, something … but I felt completely and totally normal.

Until I realized I was halfway out the door.

I sighed as I stepped out into the light rain. Thunder rumbled again, and lightning flickered over the tall buildings around me. Heavier rain was coming. Unless I wanted to get drenched, I'd better finish this quickly.

Something hard struck the back of my head. Spots of light burst in my vision. I staggered to my knees, skidding my palms on the wet sidewalk.

Eric stood next to the door, holding his dagger tight in one hand, pommel toward me. He glared. "Didn't think you'd actually be stupid enough to follow that chippy's orders."

I rose, holding my hands out. "Look, I don't want—"

He sneered at me. "Then walk back inside, and next time I come around, don't see fit to stick your nose in my business."

My chest tightened. I'd really hoped to resolve this without physical conflict. "Sorry. Can't do that."

His eyes flickered, and he lunged forward at me. I sidestepped, knocked his arm to the side. He punched me in the ribs with his free hand. I huffed out a short breath and pulled away. That'd be a bruise tomorrow.

The knife blade glittered in the lamplight as he slashed at me. I twisted and it ripped along my right bicep, stinging as it dug into flesh. Should've had my gun, but it was back in my coat pocket. Inside. *Stupid.*

Eric jived back and forth and came at me again on my wounded side. I grabbed his arm with my left hand and spun so my back was to him, the arm braced over my shoulder. He punched me in the lower back, but this close he didn't have the power for a good, solid shot.

I cracked his arm over my shoulder.

He howled. The knife clattered to the ground. I spun, pushed him away, and punched. One, two, three to his face, grabbed his hair and smashed my knee into his nose.

His head bounced like a rubber ball, and he collapsed to the ground.

I stood panting, my hands raised defensively, waiting for him to get up.

He didn't move. I walked over and knelt down beside him. The rain was washing away the blood on his face. I'd broken his nose, and probably his arm.

I grabbed his arms and dragged him into the alley off to the side of the Howler, then crouched down again and began going through his pockets. I found his wallet, but all it held was a few dollar bills. No driver's license, just my luck.

I took the bills—heck, Giselle wouldn't pay me for this job—and replaced the wallet, then finished rifling through his pockets. In Eric's breast pocket, something sharp jabbed my finger. I hissed and pulled whatever it was out of the pocket.

The dim light of the lamp revealed a small tie pin in the shape of a fairy-star flower. My heart sank. I stood and carried the pin to the mouth of the alley for a better look. The lavender enamel glimmered with a golden sheen in the rain and the lamplight.

I muttered an oath.

I returned the flower pin to Eric's pocket, propped him up against the wall so he wouldn't choke to death on his own blood, and went back inside. I hadn't seen anyone walk past during our brief fight, but apparently searching through Eric's pockets had taken longer than I'd thought, because the place had gained several new customers since I'd left.

Roe stood behind the counter where I'd left her, scrubbing the copper bar harder than looked necessary. She looked up at the jingle of the bell, and her eyes widened in surprise.

Before she could speak, Giselle hurried over to me with my hat and coat in hand. "Here, take these," she said, shoving them into my arms. She spun me around and pushed me back toward the door.

"Hey, hey," I said loudly. "C'mon, Giselle, I just beat up a guy for you, don't you think that earns me another drink?"

She raised her eyebrows and set her jaw. "You're scaring my patrons," she said in a low voice.

I didn't look away, just stared her in the eye. She stared back, blocking the door with one arm, eyes that dark burnt-sugar brown again. I clenched my teeth. Something in my chest tightened, and I realized that even though I knew Giselle had been charmin' me all these years, at some point I'd begun to think of her as a friend.

My mistake.

"Do you know who you've gotten me in trouble with?" I said in a low, terse voice. "Do you know who Eric was working for?"

She shrugged dismissively. "Thank you for taking care

of it, Owan."

"Wait, Giselle—"

She shut the door in my face.

I stared at the wooden door for a moment, anger and betrayal warring in my head as my face and neck grew warm. I closed my eyes briefly, then placed my hat on my head and walked down the street, shrugging into my coat.

I was about a block away when I heard wet, splashing footsteps behind me. I turned, my hand going to the gun in my coat pocket.

Running down the sidewalk after me was Roe, her trench coat flapping around her and an umbrella threatening to tug free from her hand. She stopped in front of me, smiled hesitantly, and said, "Thank you. For what you did. I don't know if beating him up will teach him not to come around anymore, but thank you."

I glared at her. "Thank your boss. She's the one who asked me to do it." I turned and started walking. Maybe she didn't deserve my anger. Or maybe Giselle had sent her to cozy up to me, cool me down a bit. That would just be like her.

She caught up, half-running to keep up with my long strides. From the corner of my eye, I could see her frown. "Giselle did? But that doesn't make any sense. She told me she couldn't do anything about him."

"Yeah, of course *she* couldn't," I muttered.

"Which never made sense to me, because Giselle's far more powerful than Eric."

I stopped on the street corner and turned to her. "Look, don't play a dumb Dora to me, okay? I found the lavender fairy star in his pocket."

A little wrinkle appeared between Roe's fine eyebrows. "What?"

As if she didn't know. "The pin. You know, the sign that he's part of Niall Byrne's gang?"

Roe's face went deathly pale. For a second, she looked like she was about to faint, but she put her hand on my arm and steadied herself. "Niall Byrne? But..." She lifted her hand from my arm. "You're bleeding!"

I looked at my arm. Blood had soaked through the sleeve, leaving a large red stain that was spreading with the help of the rain. "Just a small cut." I started to turn.

"Wait! Mister ..."

"Craig."

"Mr. Craig." She caught up to me again. "Let's at least bandage that up. It's not far to my place."

I eyed her. She still looked white as a ghost, the freckles on her nose and cheeks standing out against her pale skin. Her curls had started to sag from their pins with all the rain. I sighed. Maybe she really, truly didn't know that her ex-beau had been one of Niall Byrne's men. Maybe.

I held out my elbow, and she placed her hand on my good arm. We set off down the street.

ᴿOE lived in a fifth-story apartment in midtown. Instead of going through the front door, she directed me around to the back and up the fire escape. There, she pried open the window she'd left barely cracked, hiked up her skirt, and ducked into the apartment. She had nice legs.

"Curious way to get into a place," I said, climbing after her.

She blushed. "Sorry. I didn't even think. I've been switching around my paths home lately, because—" She bit off her sentence and looked away.

She's hiding from Eric.

"Besides, my next door neighbor is nosy. If she saw me bringing home a man at this hour!" Roe forced a laugh.

I looked around the modest apartment. Off to the left of the kitchen area, there was a battered white door, and a little hallway that I guessed led to the bedroom. No pictures hung on the white plaster walls, and just a threadbare sofa sat in the living room.

Roe went to one of the kitchen cabinets and pulled open a drawer. "May as well sit down. Should I get a kettle going? Do you like coffee, or tea?"

"Coffee, please." I tossed my coat and hat over the back of a chair. I rubbed my hand on the faded floral tablecloth. "So. How long ago did you move here?"

Roe started a kettle of water on the stove, collected a small leather satchel from a cabinet, and sighed as she came over to the table. "Not very long—maybe a month? Eric knew where I lived and ..." she hesitated.

Time to change the subject. "What're you doing in the Big Apple anyway? Your accent don't fit."

She snorted as she pulled a chair out beside me and sat down. "Springfield, Missouri. Is it still that obvious? I've been living here for a year."

"Still obvious, sorry."

She motioned at the long sleeve of my previously-white button-down. "I'm not going to be able to do much with that still on."

I felt the tips of my ears color. "Umm..."

"Oh please. I grew up on a farm with five brothers. Wouldn't have pegged you for such a bluenose."

"Hey, that finally sounded like proper NYC talk," I joked.

Roe laughed she began unwinding a ball of gauze. This laugh sounded easier, genuine.

I unbuttoned my vest and shirt and pulled them off, then

rolled up the sleeve of my undershirt so she could easily get at the cut. Peeling away the wet, rain-and-blood-soaked fabric pulled the wound open again. Roe pressed a wad of gauze to it as she pulled a tin of salve from the bag with her free hand.

"Okay, so, farm girl," I started, trying to distract my mind from the fact that I was sitting here in my undershirt with a very pretty fae chick. I breathed deep, relaxed my shoulders. "Why'd you move to the grand ol' NYC?"

"I'm studying antiquities."

Okay, this dame was full of surprises. "Studying antiquities" was slang for "working with relics," and I only knew one group fool enough to do that nowadays.

"You're a curator?" I asked.

She nodded.

I mimed raising a glass in a toast. "That's a crazy bit of work."

"Crazy, but necessary." She didn't sound disapproving, just firm. "There's been an influx since the Great War, and it's more necessary than ever to have a firm handle on them."

"I'd believe it."

"Have you ever encountered a relic?"

"No. But I'm not dumb. I've heard the stories." Stories of plagues unleashed by one person wearing the wrong necklace. Stories of folks' minds being taken over with just a touch. Relics were objects that had been imbued with one single-minded purpose, and they made glamour nearly irresistible to full-bloods. To humans and half-fae like me... I shuddered. Yeah, I was perfectly happy to let the curators handle those sorts of jobs.

Roe peeled the wad of gauze away from my arm and frowned at the cut. "That'll need iodine for certain." She opened the cap on a dark bottle and dabbed some iodine out on a clean piece of gauze. "How about you, Mr. Craig?"

"Me?" I grinned. "Mostly I spend my days tracking down lost puppies and errant husbands. I'm good at findin' lost stuff, you might say."

"Giselle mentioned that you were a private detective. Any police work?"

I jumped as she pressed the iodine-soaked gauze to my arm. "Ouch! Lugh's Spear, woman, you could've warned me!"

She grinned. "Aww, is the big tough shamus scared of a little sting?"

I rolled my eyes. "How long did you date Eric?"

Her movement slowed a little, and she glanced away. "A couple of months. One of the girls I used to room with set us up on a blind date. He was sweet at first, but he got really possessive after a while. Hit me once, when I went out with other friends without asking him for permission first."

I raised my eyebrows. "What'd you do?"

"Gave him a black eye."

"Sounds like growing up with five brothers was good for you."

"Thanks."

We talked a bit more as she finished cleaning up and bandaging the cut—mostly about life in New York, how she'd met Giselle, our various favorite parts about living in a big city. I couldn't help but compare her lively, cheerful personality to Giselle's ice-queen attitude. She got me coffee, and our talk drifted to our tastes in books and theater. With theater, at least, we agreed, and it took all my self-control not to ask if we could go to a play sometime. I figured that was the last thing she needed, since she was still dealin' with Eric.

After a time, I glanced at my watch and realized it was nearly ten o'clock. "I'd better go. Can't have your neighbors thinking we'll keep them up all night with our chatter."

She laughed. "The walls aren't that thin."

"Nah. I got a Rex Stout book I'd like to dig into and besides, you need sleep too." I stood, pulled my shirt back on and buttoned it up.

Roe began clearing the table, and I caught her nervously glancing at the door. Of course, her snoopy next door neighbor. I sympathized.

"Don't worry, I'll leave the same way I came in," I said. "Say, Roe, would you like me to meet you at the Howler tomorrow night? What time do you get off work? I'll walk you home."

"Oh, I don't want to inconvenience you."

"No inconvenience. I want to make sure your lousy ex got the picture."

She started to run her fingers through her hair, then winced as she got caught on a bobby pin. "I can't believe Giselle convinced you to go to all this trouble just for me. And to get yourself possibly involved with a gang ..."

I shrugged. No need to bother her by saying that I hadn't been able to resist Giselle's "request."

"Well, if you're certain, I wouldn't mind it. I'm pretty sure Eric doesn't know where I live—I've been able to slip away each time he's tried to follow me—but it wouldn't hurt." She held out her hand. "Thanks for everything, Owan."

I shook her hand, smiled. "See you tomorrow night." I pulled on my coat and hat and slipped out the window.

Roe shut and locked it behind me, then waved as I climbed down the fire escape.

The rain had stopped while we'd been in her apartment, but everything still dripped. I walked down the alley, kicking a few pebbles along in front of me as I thought.

I couldn't figure Giselle's angle. Obviously she hadn't

wanted a fight in her speakeasy, since she'd kicked us out once Eric had gotten angry. And the fact that she'd quickly shoved me out after the fight suggested that she didn't want to be associated with Eric's lesson in manners. Had she known who Eric was? It sure seemed like it. She'd been afraid to ban him from the Howler.

But why would she think that getting beat up would get through Eric's thick skull?

I sighed. I'd been in over my head the moment I'd set foot in Giselle's speakeasy, and if I could travel back five years ago and tell myself to just walk on by, that the Howler wasn't all it was cracked up to be, I'd do it in a heartbeat.

Although then I'd have never met Roe.

I snorted at myself. *C'mon, Owan. You barely met the girl, she's still dealing with a nasty ex-beau, and you're already thinkin' that 5 years of trouble was worth meetin' her? Gimme a break.*

I rounded the corner of the building, and the hairs on the back of my neck rose. I stopped. Scanned the street ahead of me. It looked empty.

It was the night for me to fulfill clichés, because I didn't even bother glancing up.

Something heavy and scratchy dropped over my head. I yelled and flailed at it, trying to drag the material—a blanket?—off of me. I could hear the muffled sound of footsteps, and the spring and creak of the metal fire escape above me. Arms wrapped around me, pinning the blanket in place. I struck backward, my elbow finding someone's ribs, drew my arm forward, and went to strike again.

A kick to the back of my knees dropped me to the ground, and another in my gut made me curl up, feeling like I was about to vomit.

I forced myself upward, wrapping an arm around my gut. Something cracked into the back of my head. My vision swirled into black.

I awoke sitting in a wooden chair, my wrists tied to the arms and my ankles bound to the chair legs. I tipped my head back and blinked hard. I sat in a corner of what looked to be a warehouse, surrounded by stacks of wooden crates and boxes. There was a small open space around me, with a desk and wooden filing cabinet to one side, like someone used this as an office in a pinch.

"Hey, boss-man, he's awake!"

I glanced right, where the voice had come from. Two men sat on overturned crates, using a third as a table to hold their cards and a lantern. Another lantern hung near the desk.

"Hey, boss!" One of the guys got up and disappeared behind the stacks of crates.

The other ignored me and proceeded to pick up his

buddy's cards and look through them.

I looked down at my wrists. Rough hemp rope pinned them securely to the chair arms—they had pushed up my sleeves, not even leaving me the wiggle room that fabric could create. I twisted my hands anyway and cringed as the rope bit into my skin.

The echo of footsteps brought my head up again, and I watched as two goons with actual swords slung at their sides stepped into the little space. Following them was a tall, slim fae wearing his curly dark hair in a ponytail.

Behind him was Eric, bruises on his face and his arm in a sling.

My heart sank to my feet.

"That him?" the taller fae asked.

Eric spat and stalked forward. "Think you're smart now, wise guy?" His fist cracked against the side of my head.

The blow knocked me to the side, rocking the chair. I tasted blood at the back of my mouth, but I shook it off and straightened. "Shame ya couldn't do that earlier tonight."

Eric drew his fist back again. And yeah, I'm not ashamed to admit that I cringed a bit. Stars burst in my vision. My head snapped to the side, and this time I stayed there. My temple throbbed in a growing headache. If he kept this up, I was gonna pass out again.

"That's enough, Eric," the tall fae said.

"But—"

"I don't need to repeat myself, do I?"

The fae's calm, cool voice sent a chill down my spine.

Eric stepped away from me, head bowed. He nodded to his boss, then turned and left the room. At a nod from the tall fae, one of the swordsmen followed Eric. I heard the *sching* of metal on leather, then the sound of ripping flesh, a strangled gasp, and a limp body hitting the floor. The swordsman came back into the room, cleaning blood off his blade.

He'd just ordered Eric killed. Just like that. I closed my eyes as shivers spidered down my back. Then I firmly pushed my fear to the back of my mind. I'd deal with it later. Now, I needed a cool mind.

The tall fae walked past me and settled on the desk, his ankles crossed as he studied me. His gloved fingers slowly tapped out a rhythm on the desk's edge.

I straightened up. "Hi. I'm Owan Craig. I'd say I'm pleased to meet you, but …" I shrugged, tried to lift my hands.

He snorted. "Yes. Owan Craig, private investigator. And I'm Niall Byrne, as I'm sure you've already guessed."

"I had a sneakin' suspicion, yeah."

Niall crossed his arms. "Care to explain why you beat up one of my men at the Howler tonight, Mr. Craig?"

I shrugged again. "Didn't like his tone toward one of the waitresses."

"Ah yes. Roe Gillam." Niall glanced at the two goons who stood by their abandoned card game. "Eric's ex-girlfriend, isn't it?"

The taller of the two men shrugged. "To hear it, boss, they're still together, she's just bein' cagey."

Niall rolled his eyes. "All this trouble over a skirt." He eyed me. "What's your score in this fight?"

"Nothin'. Giselle just asked me to help out."

Niall laughed. "And out of the goodness of your heart, you agreed? She didn't even tell you who he was, did she?"

I shook my head.

Niall nodded, smiling. "Good. I appreciate you being forthright. It'll make this a lot easier." Niall went around to the back of the desk and opened a drawer, began slowly moving aside the contents. "Do you know what my biggest import is, Mr. Craig?"

I shifted in my chair. "Not particularly. I mean, a guy in my line of work can't help but hear things, but I'd just as soon keep my nose clean and outta any gangster's business. 'Less, of course, I get hired to be nosy."

His nostrils flared, and for a second, I thought that my usual banter—be sarcastic, let the bad guys know that I knew their dirty laundry, be flippant—wasn't gonna work on this guy. Maybe I'd read him wrong. Maybe it annoyed him too much.

Niall laughed, and I sagged in relief, feeling like my limbs had gone to gelatin.

Niall plucked a long, thin bundle, wrapped in white muslin cloth, from his drawer, closed it, and walked around to stand in front of me again. He picked at a knotted string around the bundle.

"I import elfwine, Mr. Craig. You're familiar with that, surely?"

"Sure." I was bluffing. I'd heard the term, but I'd always thought it meant liquor so fine that the fae could've made it.

Niall clicked his tongue against his teeth. "And here we were being so honest with each other. That's really such a silly thing to lie about." He paused in unwrapping whatever it was in his hand and looked up at me.

"How are you doing that?" I asked. "I'm a pretty good liar. Gotta be, in my business."

"No, Owan, you're really not."

"Yeah, just go ahead and insult a guy about his job, that's fine," I muttered.

He ignored my last comment. "Elfwine is distilled in Europe, by a certain monastery in the Alps where half of the members are fae. The secret was carried with them from Tir

Ni-all when the paths were closed. The recipe has, from what I gather, largely unchanged since then, although I imagine its power has waned a bit along with the rest of our … abilities."

He finished unwrapping the object and held it up, twirling it in his long fingers. My stomach curled at the sight of the black blade coated in a thick, flaking orange rust.

Cold iron was a right nuisance to full fae, making them sick, burning them, and eventually killing them by collateral damage. Rusted iron? Rusted iron was poison to my kind. All this guy needed to do was cut me with that blade—didn't have to be a big cut either—and he could sit and watch my veins blacken. My heart would fail, and I would die gasping and in horrible pain.

Niall made no move toward me. He leaned against his desk, twirling the knife through his gloved fingers, eyes fixed on me.

I didn't like to admit it, but his intimidation was working. I balled my fists, feeling the sweat on my palms.

"So … there's a big market for elfwine, is there?" I asked, more to occupy my mind with something other than that stupid, twirling, orange-bladed knife.

Niall smiled thinly. "You'd be surprised at how much politicians are willing to pay to influence their opponents."

"Nah, I'm not. Sounds like the bloodsuckers."

Niall chuckled. "You know who else pays handsomely

for a bottle of elfwine now and again?"

The answer hit me like a freight train. I gritted my teeth, lowered my head.

"That's right, the lovely owner of the Howler, that remarkable speakeasy you seem to enjoy frequenting even though it always gets you into trouble." He twirled the knife again. "Giselle's a smart broad, I'll give her that. She knew the type of opportunity she had when she opened the Howler. Elfwine, the drink that mimics anyone's favorite liquor and slowly enthralls them."

"Just my luck," I muttered.

"So some poor, unlucky sap gets himself enthralled and is basically doing free bouncer work for Giselle," Niall continued. He stopped twirling the rusted knife and studied the blade. "And then he's asked to take care of a nuisance for one of the waitresses, because Giselle knows who the guy works for and doesn't want to ban him for fear her supply of elfwine will be cut off, but can't let him continue for fear it'll give other guys ideas. What was she hoping? That it would look like some random white knight? Or that you'd kill him?"

"She should know better by now," I muttered. Stupid. All those years being enthralled, being too lazy to actually figure out how Giselle had a hold on me. Heck, now that I thought of it, part of the enthrallment was probably to keep me from askin' too many questions.

All I could be thankful for was that I'd left my gun in my coat pocket and hadn't killed Eric. Maybe that would earn me some leniency.

Niall stabbed the knife into his desk. The *thud* made me flinch. "The problem I face now, Mr. Craig, is what to do with you. Personally, I'd be all for letting you go. But you beat up one of my men."

"Who you just killed," I said quietly.

Niall waved the comment away. "Eric was a liability. Still, if it got out that you jumped him—"

"It won't from me," I assured him. "Look, Niall, we can deal, right? Surely there are terms we could come to."

Niall studied me for a moment, his eyes half-closed as if considering. Then he straightened from the desk and left the room, his bodyguards trailing after him.

I was left alone, feeling sick and hollow.

Even though I knew Giselle had been charming me along, I'd still thought she was my friend. Some part of me had still trusted her.

I started twisting my left wrist. The rough cord chafed and tore my skin. Niall seemed reasonable for a gangster, but I wasn't about to takes chances. I didn't want to die—not here, with a gunshot to the back of the head, or in the harbor my feet bound to a sinking chunk of cement. And definitely not with rust poison seizing up my heart.

Blood streaked my wrist and I stopped, breathing hard. Panic welled in my gut. I tried to push it to the back of my mind, tried to stay calm. I'd been shot at while in the police force, and I hadn't panicked this much.

Then again, I'd never been tied up and threatened with rusted iron either.

I'd dealt with one case a few years ago where half-fae had been killed with rusted iron. I'd seen the dark, bulging veins on their bodies. The pain and terror, frozen forever in rigor mortis, on their faces. I didn't want to die like that.

Maybe if I drank elfwine that Niall Byrne gave me, my loyalty would switch to him. Should I offer that?

I immediately felt sick that I'd even thought such a thing. Giselle might be manipulative, but better be enthralled to her than to a killer like Niall.

"Owan!" The voice was a soft hiss from above me.

I whipped my head around, searching the shadows as I tugged harder on the rope around my wrists.

Roe scrambled into view on the top of a stack of crates. "Owan, stop! You're hurting yourself!"

"Roe!" I gasped. I sagged against the back of the chair and let out a strangled laugh. "How did you get here?"

"Rode on the back of the car, on the luggage rack." She clambered down, crouched beside me and starting pulling at the knots pinning my wrist.

"But how did you even hear—"

"You may not realize this, Mr. Owan Craig, but you kick up more fuss than a pair of tomcats when you're mad."

The phrasing made me laugh. "Okay, okay. Thank you." Even as I thanked her, though, my insides twisted in worry. Now I had to make sure she got out safe too. If Niall found the ex-girlfriend of his dead gang member here... I shoved the thought away.

"Thank me when we actually make it out."

After a few more seconds, the rope around my right wrist came loose. Roe moved onto my ankles as I undid the rope on my other wrist. As soon as I was free, I scrambled to my feet, then dropped back down. My legs were numb. I leaned over and started rubbing the feeling back into them.

"Roe, can you find my coat?"

"Can't you just lea—"

"That coat has my blood on it," I said sharply. "You ever been on the bad side of a fae? A blood curse is no picnic in Central Park, let me tell you."

"Oh." Roe bit her lip. "I'll look." She went around behind the desk.

I felt a little bad for barking at her, but with every second that passed, my shoulders got more tense. What would happen if we were caught?

"Here. It was half under the desk." Roe shoved it into my

arms.

I stood, slipped it on and checked my pocket. The gun was still there. I caught Roe's hand and squeezed it gently. "Sorry."

She nodded, a faint smile coming to her lips.

We slipped into the shadows of the maze of crates. Roe immediately pulled my arm to the right. Beyond the lantern sitting at the mouth of the makeshift office, the warehouse was dark, with only glimmers of light showing here and there through the stacks of crates. I was completely lost in the maze, but she guided me with confidence, our feet barely making a sound.

Roe's free hand came to my chest, pushing me to a halt. "The entrance is just here," she whispered, pointing to the end of the corridor we stood in.

I nodded and stepped in front of her, glancing around the corner.

Several guys, all dressed in the rough clothing and caps of dock workers, stood in front of the entrance, talking in low tones. One flicked a silver coin back and forth in his fingers, but the others had their hands free or in their pockets. Any one of them could be armed.

I reached into my coat pocket and gripped my pistol. Hopefully we could get past them without a shootout, but it still made me feel better.

A shout echoed from inside the warehouse. Roe gripped my hand tighter.

"It'll be okay," I whispered, and risked another glance around the corner.

The four goons had straightened, their attention caught by the shout. And it was just my luck that most of 'em were looking right where I poked my head out.

"Hey, you!" One of them yanked a gun from his belt. The others dove for various weapons in the area.

I shoved Roe back.

The shot sparked off the cement inches from my foot.

"This way!" Roe dragged on my arm, pulling me up. We ran down the aisle, and she screeched to a halt beside a smaller stack. She grabbed the straps holding the crates in place and clambered upward, wedging her feet into the cracks in the wood until she was on the top of the stack.

I scrambled after her, and we dropped down the other side to a new, narrower corridor. Footsteps rushed past on the other side of the crates.

At the opening of this corridor, a square of lamplight shone on the cement floor. Freedom was within reach.

I pulled my gun from my pocket and swung around the corner, making sure no one stood there watching for us. As I swept the open area, nothing moved.

"Okay, I think we're clear." I reached back, gripped

Roe's hand. "Ready to make a run for it?"

She nodded.

"One, two, three—" I squeezed her hand. "Go!"

We dashed for the door.

Halfway across the open floor, I spotted movement. Someone—something—running straight for Roe.

"Look sharp!" I dodged to the side and pushed her out of the way. She went tumbling.

Something struck me hard in the back, and hot spikes of pain jammed into my shoulder. I screamed. My hand went limp, and I lost the grip on my gun. My knees sagged.

I struggled, trying to see who had stabbed me.

A creature loomed over me in the lamplight, fangs bared in a mostly human face. Dark skin covered its left arm. A púca. I glanced down at the claws protruding from my shoulder. I was very lucky that it hadn't pierced an artery.

The púca began to lift me to my feet. I gasped, put my hand up to my shoulder, black tunneling my vision.

A shot rang out, and the púca lurched backward. It dropped me. I rolled to my back and pushed myself away. The púca paid no heed—its eyes were fixed on Roe, who stood across the loading bay, my pistol clutched in both hands.

"You think that bothers me, sister?" He snickered. "Try again."

"You asked," Roe said, and shot it in the chest.

The bullet knocked the púca back a few steps and to one knee. He pressed a hand to his chest, gasping.

"Owan, don't just lie there! Run!" Roe shouted.

I forced myself to my feet and staggered after her. The sounds of running steps and shouts echoed close by in the warehouse.

The street outside was muddy, slick from the rain earlier. The fish-and-refuse smell of the harbor hit me, now that I was outside and away from the sawdust in the warehouse. I glanced around. Roe yanked open the side door of a low-slung black car, scrambling inside. I ran around to the driver's side as she cranked the keys. The car rumbled to life as I slammed the door shut.

A bullet tore through the fabric roof. I yelped and grabbed Roe's shoulder, pushed her down to the seat as I worked the pedals and gearstick. The car's tires spun, then gripped, and we shot forward.

I drove fast through the maze of warehouses and buildings that made up the dockside district and didn't slow until we were on a main road, heading for my apartment. I glanced over my shoulder. There were no other vehicles on the road. I sighed and leaned back against the seat, then instantly regretted it as pain shot through my shoulder.

Roe pulled off her coat and pressed it to my shoulder.

Then she gave a strange, hiccuping gasp and covered her mouth with her hand. I glanced over. Tears rolled down her cheeks.

"Hey, hey." I reached over, out my arm around her shoulders, and gave her a gentle squeeze.

She let out a deep breath. "I …I'm sorry. I just… I shot someone."

I gripped her hand on my shoulder. "Without you, I'd probably be slowly dying from rust poison right now. Or sinking into the harbor. Thank you."

I drove in silence for a moment, watching Roe out of the corner of my eye. Her jaw was set, but as we passed the street lamps, I saw tears still glimmering in the corners of her eyes. I squeezed her hand a little more. Nothin' I could say would make it better, but just to let her know that I was there. I'd been right where she was, first time I'd shot someone.

I pulled up to the curb several blocks from my apartment and shifted in the seat. Roe's hand fell from my shoulder, and I reached up to keep her coat pressed against the wound. "I'd better get inside and take care of this."

She nodded, eyes on the floor.

"Roe." I reached for her, gently put my hand on her shoulder. "I need to ask you something."

She looked up, brushed away the tears on her lashes, and

took a steadying breath. Her makeup was smeared and her hair frizzy, but to me she looked just as pretty as she had at Giselle's speakeasy.

"First off, are you gonna be okay?"

She nodded. "It's not the first time I've shot someone. It was just ... it startled me. I didn't think I'd ever be able to hold a gun again."

Full of surprises, our little Missouri spitfire. I chuckled. "You did swell. Now, listen—Niall Byrne told me he imports elfwine. Does Giselle have elfwine in her speakeasy?"

Understanding bloomed on Roe's face. "That's why she wouldn't ban Eric."

"And she gave that elfwine to me so I'd be more compliant. So she could get work outta me for free."

Roe sighed and pinched the bridge of her nose. "Owan, I am so sorry, I didn't know ..."

"Don't be apologizin' for things your boss did." I pulled the keys from the ignition and pushed open the door, wincing. "C'mon. Let's get my shoulder cleaned up, then I'll take you home."

Without even being asked, she came around to my side of the car and put her hand on my arm. I accepted the support willingly as we walked down the street. This, I could get used to.

I spent the next two days at home, nursing my wounded shoulder and reading my new Rex Stout novel.

Or, tryin' to read, anyway.

My brain kept spinning around with the problem of what to do with Giselle's hold on me. Already I could feel an empty gnawing in my gut, something that told me that pretty soon, I'd be craving that perfect, amber-colored honey whiskey like nothing else. I even went out and bought myself a new bottle of the real stuff at another, human speakeasy. I paid through the nose for it and it didn't have nothin' on the elfwine version.

Roe came by and told me she was moving again, since Niall's men knew where she lived.

"Seems like a good idea," I told her.

Roe curled a piece of hair around her finger. She was wearing it down today, and I could barely stop myself from reaching out to run my fingers through it. She rubbed her eyes. "I can't stop thinking about how Giselle used you," she said softly. "She knew that Niall wouldn't like you roughing up one of his men."

"Funny you should say that." I straightened from my slump on the couch and winced as the stitches in my shoulder pulled. "I've gotta plan for that. Interested?"

She leaned forward, blue eyes showing a spark. "Tell me."

I told her. She laughed and said Giselle deserved it.

That night, I placed two phone calls to the police—one anonymous, and one in my official capacity as a private investigator. Then I got dressed and limped my way over to Giselle's speakeasy. Giselle greeted me as usual, eyes sparkling, a wide grin on her painted lips. She offered me a glass of my favorite honey whiskey. I accepted, put it on the bar.

"Well, baby?" She tipped her head to the side. "Not gonna drink it?"

My hands trembled, and I shoved them into my pockets. "That trash? Not bloody likely."

"Well, you're in a foul mood." She tossed a towel over her shoulder and turned, walking off. "Let me know when you've decided to be better company, baby."

I waited until she was at the other end of the bar, engaged with other customers. And then, casually, I picked up my drink, got up from my barstool, and walked over to the window.

Sure enough, there were a few more cars parked along the curb than usual, and some guys in suits were sitting along the benches and loitering on the corners.

I reached into my jacket pocket, popped the top on the lead-lined flask that I carried, and emptied the iron shavings into the lamp hanging beside the door. Sure 'nough, just as I'd thought, the golden, shimmering sparks in the air flickered. Some of them winked out. It was enough—now anyone, even full humans, could see the Howler as the speakeasy it truly was, rather than the drab storefront it masqueraded as.

Giselle's head snapped up, and she looked straight at me.

I smirked and stepped out the door. Try as she might, she wouldn't be able to weave enough glamour to cover it that quickly. Once I was outside, I raised my hand—the agreed-upon signal.

Plain-clothes detectives ran for the door, slammed it open, and poured inside, guns drawn. Shouts and screams echoed from inside. I watched the scuffle for a few minutes until two cops dragged Giselle out of the building, cuffs on her wrists. She looked over to me and bared her teeth. How had I always missed the monster under the glitz and glamour?

"Owan!" she shrieked. "How dare—help me, you worthless fool!"

I staggered forward two steps before I stopped myself. Focusing hard on keeping my feet planted, I raised the glass of elfwine and saluted her. "I am no longer your thrall, Giselle." Then I dropped the glass, allowing it to shatter across the sidewalk.

A faint golden thread appeared, stretched in the air

between us. It snapped, and I felt a gentle *pop* in my chest. She screamed again.

I turned around and walked away.

I didn't slow my pace until I got to the street corner, away from the noise and confusion. Then I stopped. There was a low, snuffling sound behind me, and it made the hairs on the back of my neck rise.

The púca stepped up beside me. Even in humanoid shape, no one would ever mistake him for a human. Too-sharp, too-long eyeteeth glittered against pale skin. He wore no hat, and his white hair was slicked back straight from his forehead, revealing the ragged points of his ears.

"Figured one of Niall's goons would be lurkin' around." I adjusted the brim of my hat against the rain nonchalantly. "What's he have to say?"

"He wished you to know that the police raid found very little, as we'd anticipated your move. But even so, he's interested in a mutual truce."

" 'Fraid I could make his life too hot for him?"

The púca snorted. "Make no mistake, Mr. Craig, Niall Byrne could order your death without blinking an eyelid. But he rather admires your ...gumption, I believe he called it. This is his offer."

"You tell your boss sure, I'll bite. Truce. But he better not come knockin' at my door, or Miss Gillam's, anytime soon."

The púca flashed his bright white teeth again. Without a word, he turned and slunk away into the shadows of the alley.

I straightened my shoulders, pushing back a shiver. No need to show that I was scared to anyone who might be watchin'.

I went across the street to the little diner where Roe waited for me. I ordered coffee at the counter, then joined her at her booth by the back window.

"Looks like you're out of a job," I told her. "Sorry about that."

"She had it coming." Roe tapped the side of her coffee cup, the tired tension evident in her hunched shoulders.

"Ya know," I said casually, "why don't you come work for me?"

She looked up, eyes widening. "What?"

"Sure. Why not? It's about time I find a partner anyway."

"You mean secretary," she said.

But I could see a small, hopeful gleam in those pretty blue eyes. "No." I blew on my coffee. "I mean partner. You've got guts, and you showed yourself pretty handy with a gun the other night. Sometimes a doll can get places a guy can't. Besides, havin' a curator—"

"In training," she corrected again.

"—would come in handy, since it looks like we're gonna get a whole lot more business with the fae now that Niall knows who we are."

"Craig and Gillam, private detectives," she mused. "I like the sound of that. Will my name be on the front door?"

"Right beside mine."

She grinned at me, her eyes twinkling, and lifted her coffee cup up to mine. "To Craig and Gillam," she said.

"To partnership."

My cup clinked against hers, and the sound echoed in my mind, pushing away the fog of the elfwine. Come what may, Roe and I could watch each other's backs, I was sure of it.

I looked up the street at the activity at the Howler and chuckled. And it sure seemed like I'd had the last word over Giselle after all.

THE SILVER BRIDLE

"So I guess I'll just make another pot of coffee, shall I?"

I looked up from the paperwork on my desk at Roe, who was standing at the little cabinet we'd wedged between her desk and the door. She shook the percolator at me, and from the rattle of the inside I could tell it was empty.

"Coffee," I repeated quietly. Then it was like an electric light popped inside my head. "Oh! Coffee. Sure, that sounds swell."

Roe smirked. "Sounds like you definitely need it. Or maybe you should go home and go to bed, boss."

I rolled my eyes as I turned back to scanning through the newspaper I held. Technically, I wasn't sure we were allowed to have the percolator or the hot plate in our little office, but the landlord hadn't yet said anything about the smell of coffee drifting down the hallway morning, noon, and night.

And with the hours we'd been pulling lately, we both needed it.

Not that we'd done anything all that *interesting*. I tossed the paper to the desk, dislodging a few more thin sheets of newsprint, and sighed. Rent was okay until the end of the month, but I was pretty sure Roe would appreciate being able to eat. I knew I would.

"No leads?" Roe asked.

I grunted.

"I know that sigh." She turned around and leaned against the cabinet, brushing a curly lock of copper hair behind a pointed ear. "It's the 'how many lost puppies do I have to find this month to pay the bills' sigh."

I chuckled at that. Roe and I had only been partners for a few months—ever since she'd quit her job at a fae speakeasy that we'd both then helped to shut down—but she already had me pegged pretty good.

Several loud knocks sounded on the outside of the door.

Roe stood, backing away from the door and glancing at me. I frowned. Anyone could see the light through the small window in the door, sure, but our hours were clearly stated on the door. It was near midnight—who would be disturbing us at this hour?

I stood and started to open my mouth to call out when I

spotted a thin silver glimmering stream of glamour coming through the keyhole in the lock.

"Roe!" I called, yanking open the side drawer of my desk.

Roe ran for her own desk.

The door slammed open just as I yanked my gun from the drawer. Three sidhé stood on the threshold of the room. Two of them were fae that I didn't recognize. One, I knew immediately. He had a pale, unnaturally shaped face, with his nose so wide and flat against his face it could almost be called a muzzle. And when he grinned, his mouthful of jagged teeth revealed him as decidedly not human or even fae.

"Evenin', Mr. Craig," he said.

"What do you want, púca?" I demanded.

He grinned broader.

Púcas—shapeshifters who changed to a horse or a dog or a panther—were fairly uncommon around here. Maybe there were more in other countries. The first time I'd met this one, he'd driven his claws through my shoulder to try to keep me from escaping his boss. The last time we'd met, he'd been delivering a threat—and a promise, that as long as I kept my nose out of Niall Byrn's business, he would keep his goons away from me.

Seeing the púca now broke that promise.

I tightened my grip on my gun even more. "I said: what do you want, crowbait?"

Out of the corner of my eye, I saw Roe's hand slowly reach for the purse sitting on her desk.

A ring of steel told me the other two goons had drawn weapons, probably knives.

The púca seemed unconcerned. "Niall wants to see you," he said.

Niall Byrne. Fae mob boss, smuggler, and someone neither Roe nor I wanted to see again.

I barked a laugh. "Sure, Niall wants to see me. Niall would probably love to help me find a nicely sized pair of concrete shoes and take me for a ride in the harbor."

The púca glanced around the office, his dark eyes glittering. "This is a nice place you have...well, for a private dick, anyway. Shame if it all...went away."

I laughed again. "Save the threats, horse-face. Niall and I had a deal. I've stayed out of his business, kept my nose clean. It's all been okay on my end. So you'd better remind your boss about it being okay on his end too."

The púca sighed. "And I'd hoped we could do this the easy way tonight."

He made a motion like he was tossing something at Roe. She yelped and ducked, and I spun around, lowering my gun to try to intercept...nothing. I had just enough time to flinch as something hit me in the neck. I dropped my gun, but too late—the thing had wrapped tightly around my neck and was squeezing.

I gasped and staggered as my vision went dark.

"Owan!" Roe caught my arm and kept me upright, though barely. "What did you do to him?"

My hand went to my neck. The rough surface of metal links met my fingers. I leaned heavily against the corner of the desk, my blood boiling. Damn púca had tricked me.

"Okay Roe," I said quietly, my voice strangely rough, even though the necklace had loosened a little now. "What's the damage?"

Roe bit the inside of her lip and glanced over at the púca.

He gestured at her. "Go on. Enlighten us, please."

Roe's ear tips flushed red before she turned back to me. Her hand pressed against the side of my neck, and my pulse jumped a bit more, pounding against her fingertips. I wondered if she'd noticed.

"It's a relic," she said quietly. "A cursed chain of some kind. I can see the ogham on the links."

Roe was training to be a curator—one of the few who study and understand relics, the ancient fae artifacts imbued with glamour. And she was a damn good one too. I wanted to question her, just to give myself a few more moments of hope, but I knew I couldn't insult her like that.

I glared at the púca.

"As I said. Niall wants to see you." The púca grinned.

I stood and grabbed my hat from the coat rack. "Well then. Let's not keep him waitin'."

THE púca took us to a seedy section of the Jersey City waterfront. The docks stretched out over the black water of the bay. Across the channel, the lights of New York City glimmered red and gold. There was probably some fae glamour in there somewhere, adding to the dazzle, but it didn't really need it.

A huddle of several men stood next to a pier under one of the street lights. One, tall and lanky with a tail of dark hair trailing down the back of his overcoat, I recognized as Niall Byrne.

Roe shivered. The night was a bit nippy, but not that cold. I reached over and put my arm around her shoulders.

Niall left the group of men and walked back towards us. His sharp fae features looked even less human in the uneven shadows of the street, and I held back a shiver of my own. He grinned at us. "Mr. Craig. Miss Gillam. Wonderful to see you again."

"Save the small talk for the fish, Niall," I said shortly.

"What do you want? I thought we had a deal."

Niall's dark eyes glanced at Roe. She raised her chin and crossed her arms.

Niall chuckled. "Fine then." His almost-Gaelic accent was more pronounced than the last time I'd met him.

What was so troubling that he let it slip now?

"Two hours ago, four of my men were attacked." Niall gestured to the side of the pier, where a set of stairs led down to what I assumed was a smaller dock. "One of them got away, although he is...injured."

"A family squabble over your latest elfwine import?" I asked, plastering a concerned smile on my face.

Niall gave me an icy look. "Would you like to interview the witness first, or view the carnage?"

The way he said 'carnage' gave me pause. It wasn't a word I would have thought Niall, a man used to violence, would say in such a grave tone.

I turned to Roe.

She shrugged. "Personal preference?" She said to Niall. "I'd rather not be here at all. But you didn't exactly give us a choice, so let's just get this over with."

"Oh yeah," I said. "That reminds me." I tugged the thick links of the chain around my neck out of my coat collar with my thumb. On the drive here, Roe had let me borrow her compact mirror so I could examine the necklace for myself. It was made of links as thick as my pinky finger and sat right against my collarbone. I could see the glamour emanating from it, an ever-present faint mist at the edges of my vision.

Niall grinned. "Now that's an interesting development, isn't it, Mr. Craig?" He cocked his head towards Roe. "Couldn't your pet curator tell you what that was?"

"I'm no one's pet," Roe snapped.

"Well. Maybe once you complete your training, we can change that."

"You reek of death and destruction and your own ruin, Niall. I'd sooner—"

Niall's hand twitched as if he was going to slap Roe. I reached forward and caught Roe's elbow, ready to jerk her away from him, but Niall met my gaze. His eyes slowly flickered, threads of gold shooting through his black irises. The *d'anam fueinneog*, the soul window of the fae. We were forever cursed to show our emotions in our eyes, unless we kept careful, tight rein on ourselves.

The last time we'd met, Niall's eyes had remained a steady, flat golden-brown. He'd been smooth talk and careful threats. He hadn't laid a hand on me or Roe himself, as if he didn't want to stain his fingers with our blood. He still hadn't laid a hand on us, but that twitch...

He was jittery tonight.

That meant we needed to be careful.

"Okay, okay," I said. "Let's hear it. What do you want us for? You've got some kind of scheme in mind."

Behind me, I heard the púca say in a low sing-song voice, "Changed your tune, didn't you."

I ignored him.

Niall nodded. "Find the man who did this to me. Who killed my men. Until you do, that cursed necklace will slowly tighten around your neck. You have twenty-four hours until it gets too tight for you to breathe."

I sighed. "Was that step really necessary?"

Niall smiled tightly. "I don't know, Mr. Craig—you tell me. Would you have come if I'd asked politely?" Without waiting for an answer, he turned and walked away, tucking his hands into his pockets.

I snorted and turned to the púca. "Looks like you're the tour guide, schmuck. Lead on."

The púca rolled his eyes and wordlessly led us to the stairs. He pulled a flashlight from his pocket and offered it to me. I flicked it on. A set of dilapidated steps led down to a long, narrow dock closer to the water, as if it was made for a motorboat. It stretched along the retaining wall out of sight of the flashlight beam.

The dark wood of the steps was spattered with blood. I carefully stepped around it. Niall's men didn't follow us down.

A tangle of...something...lay at the edge of the wood. The stink of blood and offal was thick in the air, making it difficult to breathe.

Roe coughed and dug a handkerchief out of her pocket, pressing it to her nose and mouth.

I didn't want to move forward. But I did anyway, holding the flashlight low.

A tangle of flesh lay on the edge of the dock, dripping into the water. Limbs, I thought. It was so mangled that it was hard to tell if any of it had once been human.

Roe flicked on her own flashlight—she must have gotten it from one of Niall's goons—and looked away from the carnage, searching along the back of the dock. I let her. I couldn't ask her to look any closer. I crouched down, forcing myself to scan along the blood and mess. Some bite marks on what I thought had once been an arm caught my eye. Whatever had done this, it was big.

"Well?" the púca called down.

I turned to him. "You said there were three men?"

He nodded.

"Doesn't look like three men."

He shrugged.

I shone my flashlight up and down the dock, but nothing

caught my eye. Smears of what might have been footprints streaked the blood along the dock towards the stairs, but there was nothing usable. I sighed, feeling my throat tighten as if the necklace was already strangling me. I just hoped the witness could give us more to go on.

"I've seen enough." Roe stepped to my side and gently nudged me with her elbow.

When I glanced down at her, she winked.

She'd found something. Something she didn't want Niall's goons to know she'd found.

I held back a grin.

As we met the púca back at the top of the stairs, I clicked the flashlight off and handed it back to him. "So. You have any insight as to what happened here?"

"Thought that's what you were supposed to be doing."

I shrugged. "Well, your boss wasn't all that forthcoming."

"Stuff like this, it's bad for business. Of course he's gonna be in a rotten mood." The púca shrugged back. "It's not like it's a hit or something, though."

I nodded, but kept my thoughts to myself. If it was a mob hit, it had been done by a particularly sick individual. Though personally, my bet was on some kind of monster. Which meant that if it had been a hit, it was one of the other

Sidhé mobs. And that posed its own problem. A gang war wasn't any good for anyone—especially if the gangs were Sidhé. And especially if one of those gangs had finagled a deal with something with big, sharp teeth.

The púca led us into the warehouse. Almost as soon as we stepped inside, he turned and opened a door into a small office. Three men looked up at our entrance. One was hunched in a chair, and the other two had been leaning over him. A tangle of bloody gauze lay next to an open first aid kit on the desk, and on a table to the side of the three stood an open, unlabeled bottle of booze and an empty glass.

"Walker, you up for a chat?" the púca asked.

The man in the chair nodded weakly.

"Great. Tell these two what you saw."

Walker's face paled even further. I glanced over his face, noting the lack of *d'anam fueinneog* in his eyes. No points to his ears. He was human. I'd heard that sometimes humans who spent a good deal of time among fae sometimes developed immunities to Sidhé glamour, but between his blood and the shock of the attack, I wasn't betting on much.

Walker straightened a bit, and I saw the bloody hand wrapped in bandages.

"We'd come back from a trip across the harbor. Manhattan. Delivery." Walker's voice was slurred.

I wondered how much they'd given him to drink...and

what nightmares they were trying to drown out of him.

Walker cleared his throat and continued. "Just a few—"

The púca cleared his throat.

Walker stopped for a minute. Too bad. I'd been looking forward to knowing what Niall had been smuggling over to Manhattan.

"We were just mooring the boat when this...thing...burst out of the water and lunged onto the dock. It tore through the men closest to the water faster than I could think." He shuddered.

"What did it look like?" I prompted, when it seemed like he was done talking.

"Black skin. Slick and oily. Big, sharp fangs and hooves."

"Hooves?" Roe repeated.

Walker nodded. "It came after me and I dodged to the side, but...my hand hit it in the side, and...I *stuck* to it. It couldn't turn around and get me with the hooves or the fangs, so it plunged back into the water. I couldn't get free. But I had my boot knife, and I..."

My stomach churned. He'd cut his own fingers off.

Walker's eyes glazed over, and he hunched forward again, staring at the floor.

"Walker?" Roe said softly.

He didn't answer her. Instead, he shut his eyes and

started shaking.

"We have enough," I said. "Let's go." I left the office and headed for the warehouse door. Roe's hand found mine and squeezed my fingers tightly. I squeezed her hand back, feeling her slight tremble.

"You know what happened?" the púca demanded.

I turned around and sighed. "Look, bub, it's got to be 2 am. Both Roe and I are beyond tired, and we just saw something absolutely horrific. I think we have some solid ideas to go on, but don't go expectin' miracles, ok?"

The púca nodded and let us walk out of the warehouse. The car they'd brought us in was still there, and the driver gestured Roe and me inside.

We didn't talk on the ride home, but as soon as Niall's car pulled away from the curb, Roe looked at me and said quietly, "It's a kelpie."

"Big fangs, hooves, sticky skin?" I started walking. "Sure sounds like a kelpie to me."

"Where are you going?" Roe asked, catching up with me.

"Home. I need sleep. And so do you."

"So you don't want to see what I found?"

I stopped. Roe kept walking and smiled coyly at me over her shoulder.

"It's all right, I understand. You're probably so *tired*..."

I had been, until she'd said that. I caught up with her and nudged her with my elbow. "Okay, okay. Spill the beans, bearcat."

Roe laughed and produced a ring from her pocket.

I picked it up and examined it in the glare of a streetlight. It had the weightiness of real gold to it. The band was simple, unadorned on the outside. The inside had a few faint markings, but the streetlight wasn't nearly bright enough for me to make them out in detail.

"What do you think?" I asked Roe.

"Well, it's not a relic."

I nearly fumbled the ring and looked at her. Roe grinned up at me mischievously.

""What?" she said, all innocence. "I wouldn't have let you touch it with your bare skin if it was a relic."

"Still." I handed the ring back to her. "I'm *so* glad you waited until I was holding it to announce that." I waited a beat, then added, "Doll."

Roe's eyes flashed a vivid blue. "Careful, Owan," she said. "A guy could get into trouble that way."

I grinned at her. It was probably hazardous to my health, but damn if I didn't like seein' her eyes flash and her spine stiffen. The little Missouri bearcat had a spunk to her that was beautiful to behold.

Roe rolled her eyes and pocketed the ring. "Did you see

the maker's mark on it?"

I nodded.

She rubbed her hands together. "I'll get on that."

"Tomorrow," I stressed.

"Yes, yes, yes. Tomorrow." We arrived at the corner of Roe's street, and she turned toward her apartment building. I waited at the corner until she disappeared into the front door, then turned and headed towards my own apartment several blocks away.

THE next morning, after making a few phone calls to some people Roe knew, we walked into Medford & Sons, a nice little jewelry shop just off Broadway, with black paint on the door and gold lettering on the sign. Inside, the tiled floor was swept clean, and the display cases sparkled nearly as much as their contents.

"Hello, may I help you?" The man behind the counter called.

I gave him a quick once-over. He was on the shorter side, with pointed ears, slightly bigger than a fae's, and his eyes were wide and round, the color of the irises nearly filling them completely. A clurichaun. To be honest I shouldn't have been surprised—as long as it involved gold or wine, clurichauns were sure to be involved.

His eyes met mine, then skittered away. He did the same

thing to Roe, then fidgeted with his collar. Nervous, fussy—judging by the way his eyes had lingered on the cuffs and collars of my well-worn coat, he probably already knew we weren't here to buy.

He adjusted his cufflinks and cleared his throat. "Is there something I can help you, em, find, perhaps? A simple gold locket, perhaps?"

Yeah, just like I figured. I dug into my pocket and extended the ring over the counter. "No, but if you could tell us who this belongs to, I'd be pleased as punch."

"I'm not a pawn shop," he blustered.

Roe grinned at him. "Right, you're not, and we know that. But it would sure be nice if you could help us locate the owner of this ring." She let a tiny hint of southern drawl drip into her words.

The clurichaun straightened his cuff links again, eyes widening slightly as he took Roe in. He smiled broadly, then slipped on a pair of white gloves and took the ring from me. He produced a loupe from somewhere on his person and screwed it into his eye.

At this point I had to fight not to roll my eyes. If he thought he would get Roe to buy somethin' by wheedlin' up to her, he was dead wrong. I turned and leaned against the counter, watching the door of the place as people strolled past the huge open windows. Why did jewelry shops always have such big windows? It was practically inviting the crooks to come visit some night.

I was about to say that I was gonna go down to the diner at the street corner and get myself a cup of coffee rather than wait in the jewelry shop any longer when the clurichaun cleared his throat, a fussy little *hem-hem* noise I'd never heard the like before in my life.

I glanced over my shoulder but decided to let Roe take point on this one.

Roe smiled encouragingly at him. "Did you find something?"

"Well. Yes. As a matter of fact." The clurichaun reached under the counter and pulled out a ledger, then flopped it open on the counter. Somehow, he'd opened it nearly to the right spot—he only had to turn on page and give a quick glance over the page before stabbing an entry. "Yes. This is it. About six months ago, a young couple came in and bought a matching set. They came in together the first time and then he picked it up on his own a few weeks later."

He looked up at Roe and his cheeks bunched into a smile. "See?" He used his pinky finger to point to the inside of the ring. "Just opposite my marker's mark, there—they didn't want anything fancy, bless them, but those are their initials intertwined there, in the shape of a horseshoe—the young man was raised on a horse farm, I suppose, horses were rather important to them. She was wearing a horseshoe-shaped necklace too. Very pretty." He placed the ring back down on the counter.

Roe and I exchanged a look. I didn't say it, but half of me was sure we'd found the right people. The other half of me thought that that many horseshoes was a bit on the nose.

"Where did you say you found this?" the clurichaun asked.

I glanced over at him. The squinty-eyed peepers he aimed at me told me immediately that he was suspicious. A bit late in the game, buster. I reached across to pick up the ring, but he was quicker and slid it closer to him.

"Look, pal," I said, trying to keep my tone friendly. "We just want to return the ring to them."

"Well, I have his address here, so, em-em, thank you for your service, and I can take care of the rest."

I blew out an irritated breath.

Beside me, Roe suddenly leaned forward. "I think I might be interested in a little something after all," she told him. Her elbow brushed against mine as she leaned forward. The electric tingle of glamour skittered across my skin. The hairs on my arms and the back of my neck rose. She tucked one hand under her chin, her neck arched slightly and her eyes fixed on the clurichaun with a faint, coy smile on her lips.

I eased away. Roe was full fae, sure, but I'd never seen her turn on the charm quite like *that* before. The poor little clurichaun didn't have a chance. He nearly went cross-eyed, murmured something in assent, and drifted to one of the other display cases. I waited until I was sure Roe had his full attention and that he wasn't going to even look at me, then quickly spun around his ledger and found the place he'd tapped his finger.

Allan Dulluhan, the name read. And an address near the edge of town.

I snorted softly. Dullahan. The name of the headless horseman of legend—not exactly a kelpie, but definitely fitting the horse-adjacent theme. The guy wasn't even trying to be subtle.

I copied the address down and slipped out the door.

About a quarter of an hour later, Roe came to find me at the little cafe down the street where I'd holed up. I was leaning on the corner of the door, flipping through one of the copies they had on the counter of the morning paper, but put it down as she walked up. "How'd it go?"

"I nearly had to promise to buy a bracelet, so I hope whatever you got was worth it."

Out of the side of my eye, I noticed the waitress behind

the counter looked a little *too* interested in our tête-a-tête. I offered Roe my elbow, and we sauntered down the street a ways before I pulled the slip of paper from my pocket and handed it to her.

Roe arched an eyebrow. "This is in Brooklyn, near the water."

"Sounds like a perfect place for our bruno, don't you think?"

"That it does." Roe handed me back the paper. "Let's get some lunch first. I'm starving."

THANKS to our late start to the morning, by the time we got done with 'lunch' and had made our way to the subway and across the channel to Brooklyn, the fall day had nearly used up all its daylight. The address listed was an apartment complex a few blocks from the water that looked like it housed mostly middle-class families. We made our way up three flights up stairs and knocked on the door.

The door was opened by a petite girl—no, a woman. At first glance, she was so small and delicate that I'd mistaken her for a teenager. But she couldn't be too much older than a teen, surely no more than her early twenties.

Her dark hair was pulled back in an updo, the tops of her ears concealed. But given that there was no swirling of the bright blue irises of her eyes, I had to guess she wasn't Fae.

"Can I help you?" She asked, darting a nervous glance between me and Roe, then back to me.

"Missus..." I let the title drop into a question.

"Dullahan." Her lips quirked into a little smile that quickly disappeared. "You can call me Missy."

"Missy. Do you mind if we come in for a minute?" Roe asked.

Missy briefly looked at me again.

"Missy." I dipped my hand into my pocket and pulled out the ring. I waited a brief second, long enough to see the quick glimpse of recognition on her face before I said, "We need to speak to you and your husband. Is he here?"

"No." Missy shook her head. "No, he's not here, but..." she glanced to the side, out the window at the darkening sky. "He should be home soon. I—" She caught herself, her eyes widening. "I'm so sorry! Please, come in." She pulled the door open and stepped out of our way.

The interior of the apartment was nice, if not posh. A combination kitchen and living room was decorated with pretty rugs on the wood floor and a couch and a couple of chairs under the living room windows. A door at the back of the apartment led to what I assumed was the bedroom. Small, but neat, with plenty of room for a young couple.

Missy asked us to sit and busied herself making coffee in the kitchen. Roe and I sat down on the couch as we introduced ourselves. We didn't have to wait long. Before Missy even had the coffee to us, the doorknob rattled, and a man stepped into the apartment. He was tall, a head taller than me, muscles evident even though his loose checked shirt and dungarees. A guy like that could pick me up by the collar and pitch me out the window.

The man froze on the doorstep, the knob of the door clutched in his hand.

Missy said through gritted teeth, "Allan. Why don't you come in?"

"Who..." Allan looked to us, then Missy, his shoulders hunching in. His eyes darted around the room as if he suspected someone to be hiding behind the curtains.

"These are Owan Craig and Roe Gillam, a couple of private detectives. They have your ring, Allan."

I concealed a wince. Would've preferred to tell him that myself, if I was honest. I stood up and gestured to the man. "It was turned in at the docks. We were just trying to locate the owner, Mr. Dullahan."

The words didn't seem to calm the man down. If anything, he looked even more like a trapped rat. I glanced over at Roe. She frowned slightly. I agreed. This was not how I expected a kelpie to act.

Most sidhé were...confident. Cocky, even. They knew they had abilities humans did not and saw themselves as predators on top of the food chain. But this guy was...if I was honest, he was acting guilty.

"No worries Alan. We just have a few questions that we wanted to ask you."

Alan stared at us suspiciously, his eyes darting wildly from Roe to me, then to Missy, then back to us. For a second, I was afraid that he would spin around and run out the door. I braced, ready to go run after him. But instead he slowly shut the door behind him, coming to sit down on the couch.

Missy brought coffee and placed it on the coffee table, but instead of sitting beside her husband, she stood beside the couch, hands knotted in her apron.

"What's this about?" Allan asked, looking between me and Missy.

"As I said before, we just wanted to ask you some questions and—" I held up the ring that caught his eye. "You obviously recognize this, so let's not beat around the bush."

Missy was staring at him with a look that I didn't like. Gone was the timid girl that Roe and I had met at the door. She seemed tense, almost angry. The tension between them was so thick I could have cut it with a knife. And the way that Alan shrank from her gave me pause. I couldn't quite figure out the dynamic between the two of them. It seemed odd that Alan, who had at least a head and shoulders and several inches on Missy, would be the one who was jumpy.

But that would make sense then, wouldn't it, if he was the one who had killed those men at the docks.

I waited, but neither of them offered any information. Before I could say anything Roe said, "Allan, this ring was turned in down at the docks this morning."

I caught on to what she was doing immediately, and nodded. "Yes, it was found by a dock worker early this morning and turned in at his office. We were hired to find the original owners, as no one recognized it."

Something in Allan's manner seems to relax a little. He looked back and forth between us, and his shoulder straightened a little from their hunched position.

"Would you mind telling us how it got there? Just so we can follow up with our employer, make sure there was no stolen property involved," Roe said.

I glanced over at Missy. She still stood primly upright at the side of the couch, her eyes on Allan. Her hands were no longer knotting her apron, but fine lines carved into her face at the sides of her mouth, signaling a frown just as surely as if her mouth had been turned downward. And if her shoulders got any tenser, they'd be up around her ears. Her eyes smoldered with some strong emotion I couldn't quite label. "Yes, Allan," she said, her voice brittle. "Please tell us."

Allan leaned towards, elbows on his knees, as if he

couldn't face looking at his wife. "I...I gave it to my cousin. We've been having some money troubles and he told me he knew a guy who could get me a good price for it."

Missy's shoulders eased down a bit.

"I didn't want to tell you..." Allan's voice faltered. "I'm sorry."

Missy started to say something, then checked herself. Instead, she just nodded.

I raised my eyebrows, tryin' to figure out a good way to say that was about the most ridiculous load of malarkey I'd ever heard, but instead, Roe reached over and caught my arm.

She stood. "Well, thank you for clearing that up. We should go report to Mr. Byrne, Owan, and let him know we found the ring's rightful owner."

I gave her a startled glance, but she just raised her eyebrow and nodded towards the door.

"My partner is correct. Thank you for your cooperation," I said to the couple.

Missy stood and saw us to the door. "We appreciate you returning the ring so much," she said quietly, her voice calm and almost meek once more.

"Of course. And if we can be any further assistance—"

"I'm quite sure we can sort it out from here." Missy all

but slammed the door in my face, leaving me staring at the wood panels for a moment, trying to get my brain to catch up with how neatly I'd just been swept out the door.

I looked at Roe as I turned to retrace my steps to the front door. "Well, that was something."

"Something is...a word for it," Roe said. She held up her finger to her lips, then I saw a flicker of glamour around her form, outlining her curves. For a split second she almost seemed to fade from view, then solidified.

I almost asked her what she was doing, then realized...she'd used her glamour to turn herself invisible. I could still see her, but that was because I was looking straight at her. If I'd been looking away and not known what she'd done, I wouldn't have been able to find her unless she wanted me to.

I walked away, continuing to talk and making my tread a little heavier than usual, hoping that if Missy was listening, she'd be fooled into thinking that both Roe and I were leaving. I'd have stayed, but as a half fae, my glamour wasn't nearly as strong as Roe's.

So, for the second time that day, I found myself kicking my heels while I waited for Roe. I didn't mind too much. All things considered, she was the perfect partner. I mean, a whip-smart dame who could disappear at will so she could eavesdrop on suspects? What private investigator wouldn't give his left eye for that kind of help?

I lingered on the corner of the stairs two flights down in the building—close enough I could hear Roe if she shouted for help, but far enough away that no one would associate me with that particular apartment. I got a few glares from a couple of folk who passed up or down—one a fresh guy who stopped and stared at me as if he hoped to intimidate me out of my corner spot. I just stared back at him and after a bit he dropped his eyes and moved on.

At last, I heard the familiar gait of Roe's heels coming down the stairs.

"What'd you get?" I asked.

She caught my elbow and pulled me down the stairs after her. "I'll tell you when we get on the street."

We passed a couple of old biddies chatting in the lobby, who clucked their tongues at how scandalously close Roe and I walked. I ignored them and kept going, focused on how stiff Roe felt next to me. What had scared her that she was this worried?

She didn't speak until we'd turned the corner, then she leaned her head back and blew out a deep sigh of relief. "Something's wrong there, Owan," she said quietly. "Something's *really* wrong."

"What did you hear?" I asked again.

"Once they thought we had left, Missy started shouting at Allan—it was all garbled, but I'm pretty sure she was swearing at him. My grandmother would've said she sounded distinctly not ladylike." Roe chuckled a bit, then sobered again. "And then I heard someone get hit."

"Allan hit Missy?" I asked.

"No...I think that Missy hit Allan."

I paused and looked over at Roe, frowning. "That little girl took out a man half again her size?"

"She's hardly a girl, and let me finish." Roe shook my arm. "So he slammed up against the door, and it rattled so hard I thought it would fall off the hinges. And then I heard Missy slap him again, and he said, 'I'm sorry! I'm sorry, I'll never do it again!' And she hissed, really quietly, 'I'll kill you if you even so much as think about leaving me again, Allan.'"

We were silent for a minute as we walked. I chewed over Roe's report. Had we had it wrong? When I'd first laid eyes on Missy, my bet had been that she was the human, somehow kept under thrall—or just terrified into staying—by her husband, the kelpie. But...was Missy the kelpie? Was Allan, the human, covering for her?

"What do you think that means, Roe?" I asked.

She shook her head. "I don't know. This whole thing is

so mixed up. Maybe the ring doesn't mean anything—maybe one of the men at the dock bought it from a pawn shop, or had stolen it. Maybe Allan and Missy are just two people with a troubled marriage. And even if one of them was the kelpie...would we *really* turn them over to Niall?"

I caught her meaning straight away. The kelpie, whoever it was, *was* a killer. They deserved being brought to justice. But Niall was also a criminal—and he was *cruel*, besides. He'd once threatened to poison me with rusted iron, which would've been a death sentence for me—just for stickin' my nose where it didn't belong.

It would be better for everyone if we turned the kelpie over to the police, though for that we'd need a sight more evidence.

Couldn't imagine Niall would be too understandin' of our reasoning there, though.

As if on cue, the necklace around my neck tightened a bit. I winced. It had been getting tighter all day, chafing like an uncomfortable collar, but until now, I'd been able to ignore it. Now, with a pinching sensation, I could feel it shrink down again, just enough that it dug into my throat.

"Owan?" Roe looked up at me, concern in her bright blue eyes.

"I'm fine," I said, just managing to keep my voice from croaking.

It was now dark enough that the street lamps were coming on. A golden halo surrounded each globe, showing the gathering fog as the wind swept inland from the ocean.

As we turned away from the shoreline to head toward the subway station, I paused. When Roe started to ask me what was wrong again, I held up my hand, shushing her.

The sound came again—a wet clopping sound, like a horse trotting through a puddle. Roe and I glanced at each other, eyes wide, and without a word we turned and ran.

The streets were even more fog-shrouded now, deserted even though the hour wasn't that late, and echoing from the building around us was that damned clopping as whatever was chasing us—the kelpie, most like—picked up its pace as well. It clattered in my ears, and before too long I could hear the huffing of breath.

I turned. There, bearing down on us with the fog swirling around its form, was the kelpie. Black, oily fur rippled over thick muscle. Its lips pulled back in a rictus grin, pointed teeth streaming foam and slobber.

Roe caught my sleeve and dragged me into an alley. She pulled her pistol from the holster under her coat. I followed her lead, my panting making the barrel waver as I aimed it at the entrance of the alley.

The kelpie came around the corner. In the glow of a

close street light, I could see drops of oily water streaming through its mane, dripping onto the brick streets.

"What do we do?" Roe whispered to me.

I risked a quick glance behind me. The alley stretched long and straight behind us. If we bolted, the kelpie would run us down before we reached the end.

"Back up," I whispered to her. "Slowly."

We began to edge down the alley.

The kelpie lowered its head and huffed. In the dark silhouette it presented against the street lights, I couldn't see its eyes, but I had no doubt it was watching us very, very carefully.

Suddenly it dashed forward.

Roe and I fired at almost the exact same time. The sound of the shots echoed off the bricks around us. The kelpie snarled and stumbled. I fired again, this time taking more precise aim.

The kelpie's back leg buckled, and it tumbled forward. As it rolled, it suddenly shrank, the dark fur disappearing, replaced with pale, freckled human skin.

Roe made an embarrassed noise and turned away.

I stared at the body lying on the ground in front of us. "Allan. Fancy meeting you here."

Allan glanced up at me, grimacing as he pressed his hand to the bullet wound in his calf. "How—"

"Silver bullets. The little buggers work wonders like you wouldn't believe." I hadn't been completely certain the silver bullets would halt his ability to hold his kelpie form, but I'd hoped that it would at least sting a bit more than usual and maybe make the kelpie think twice about attacking us.

Allan let out a sharp laugh. "Well done."

I leaned down and offered my hand. "Let's get you up and decent, and then find a place to talk."

Allan's eyes snapped to me, widening in surprise. "You—I thought you'd just kill me."

"We don't work like that," Roe said. "Now hurry up. I'm getting a crick in my neck from standing this way."

I chuckled and shook my hand. "C'mon, Allan. This offer won't last forever."

Allan suddenly grabbed my hand. His eyes locked on mine. "Just do one thing for me. I'll tell you everything, but then...you have to help me get away from Missy. Please."

Out of the corner of my eye, I could see Roe frown.

I merely shrugged."Let's see what you have to say."

Allan hesitated, then said softly, "I guess it's better than nothin'."

Once I'd gotten him standing, I shucked my coat and tossed it to him. He pulled it on and belted it tightly.

"You're safe, Roe," I said. "No need to be shy, doll."

If looks could kill, the one I got from her would have put

me in the ground in ashes.

"Back to the office?" she asked.

"Seems like the best place," I said.

Allan was silent as we made our way back to the office, his limp becoming more and more pronounced as blood trickled down his bare leg. I'd feel more sorry for the guy, but he *had* tried to kill us...or at least take a big bite out of my skin. And even if it did hurt, leaving the bullet in his leg was better for everyone, since the silver prevented him from shifting to his kelpie form.

I made no effort to coax him to talk, and neither did Roe. We got him into the office with no issue, though both of us had to help him maneuver the stairs—by that time, his face was drawn and pale. I tucked the extra chair in the corner between the two desks and pulled it out, then opened the bottom drawer of my desk. Sure enough, I still had a few clothes left over from the time I'd used the place as both office and apartment. At the moment, they were only serving as cushions for the bottle of Scotch—the real stuff, not the bathtub gin dosed with food available at every speakeasy. I pulled them out. They needed a good ironing, but for our purposes, they would work.

Roe left to get water for the percolator in the washroom at the end of the hall. As Allan dressed, I busied myself by hanging up Roe's wet coat, tossing my fedora on the corner of my desk, loosening my tie, and reclaiming my own coat from Allan.

"You have one too."

I turned around at Allan's words. He gestured to the necklace, now tight against my throat.

"Excuse me?" I said.

He pulled something from the neck of the borrowed shirt. A horseshoe pendant on a thin silver chain, just as the clurichaun at the jewelry shop had said...

No. Not a horseshoe. I squinted.

"It's a bridle bit," Allan said quietly.

I raised an eyebrow. Well now. That was interesting. He started to speak, but I shook my head.

"Let's wait until Roe gets back. No use in using more words than you have to."

It didn't take Roe but a minute to come back and start the coffee up on the hotplate. Then we took our places—she hitched herself up on the edge of my desk, and I leaned beside her. Allan sat in the chair, elbows on his knees, looking up at us.

"Well?" I said, breaking the silence.

Allan looked at the ground, fiddling with the bridle necklace. "I was born in upper New York state," he said quietly. "Came to New York when I was a teenager to work

in the construction business. Missy was a shopgirl. She—
we—we dated for a while. I got to where I trusted her. Told
her my secret."

"That you're a kelpie," Roe said.

Allan nodded.

"And she just believed you?"

"She...didn't, at first. I showed her...and...I don't know,
she seemed to take it in stride alright. There were some
questions. Some...problems. But she seemed alright with it
after she'd had a couple of weeks to think it over. We went
shopping for rings at this little jewelry store I'd found. It's
owned by a clurichaun." He snorted out a desolate sounding
laugh. "But I guess you already knew that."

I nodded.

"We ordered matching rings. And shortly after we were
engaged, Missy bought us these." Allan held his necklace up
for Roe to see. "Mine's a bridle bit. Her's is a horseshoe. I
thought it was kind of silly, but Missy thought it would be
sweet, and... I couldn't tell her no. She has this way of
wrapping me around her little finger... even now." He ran his
hand through his dark curls, slicking water out of them.
"Even when I know what she's really like."

Roe gave me a look. I nodded back. The argument Roe
had overheard certainly made more sense now. I had a
feeling that Allan wouldn't appreciate us bringing it up...at

the same time, would it help if we commiserated with him?

Roe said, "So what does the necklace do? May I look at it?"

Allan gave her a startled look.

"I'm training as a curator," Roe assured him. "I know how to handle relics."

"I...don't think it's a relic," Allan said reluctantly. "It's only a year old."

"Does it have ogham on it?"

"I don't know. I can't take it off, and I didn't pay attention to the chain when I first put it on." Allan looked at the ground and murmured, "I don't know if I'd know ogham if I saw them, anyway. My family was more concerned with fitting in with human society than keeping up the traditions from our heritage."

Had to admit that I was feeling sorry for the kid. I pushed the thoughts away. Maybe he was telling the truth, and maybe he wasn't. All I knew for sure was that silver bullet in his leg was the only thing keeping him from shifting to his kelpie form, and I sure as hell wasn't removing it until we knew he wouldn't harm us.

Roe approached Allan, and I stiffened, ready to leap forward at the first sign of trouble. From her pocket, Roe pulled a pair of thin leather gloves. Smart—touching relics with bare skin was just asking for trouble.

Allan lifted his chin, and she picked the bridle charm from his chest, looking at the front and back of it. Then she straightened and walked around behind him, examining the links of the fine chain as she did so. After a moment, she shook her head and went to her desk. She took a small satchel out of the bottom drawer, the same one I'd seen her carrying when she arrived after her... lessons or classes or whatever they were—and removed a magnifying glass from it.

Allan straightened up, his shoulders tense, his back stiff and straight, as Roe lifted the chain from the back of his neck once more. After a moment of Roe studying the chain under the magnifying glass, she shook her head.

"They're there," she told me. "Tiny, but they're there."

Allan groaned, and the stiffness went out of his spine. He folded forward, head in his hands.

"What are they exactly?" I asked Roe.

She pursed her lips. "Ogham of binding, control, subjugation. Without being able to see Missy's necklace, I can only take a guess, but I bet it allows her to control when he shifts."

"And I don't always remember what happens," Allan said quietly. "I don't think that's an effect Missy had planned on, but it certainly didn't bother her."

Roe's lips tightened, and I winced. So it was pretty

possible that Allan had no memory of coming after us just now, or of killing Niall's men. So why had Missy sent him after them, anyway?

I said, "I take it you want out of this."

"Of course I want out of this," Allan growled. "I don't want to keep—" He suddenly went tense, his words cutting off in a strangled growl of pain. He grabbed the bridle pendant, tugging on the chain, which was now glowing around his neck. His skin rippled, a slick hairy pelt spreading over his arms before retracting.

I stared, momentarily caught off guard.

Roe rushed forward, slipping her gloved hand under the hot chain. The smell of burning leather replaced the smell of searing flesh.

"Roe!" I glanced around the room, trying to find something to get between the chain and Allan's neck, anything other than Roe's hand.

Before I could find anything, the glow faded. Allan gasped and closed his eyes, teeth gritted. Roe removed her hand and flexed her fingers, wincing.

I crossed the room and caught her wrist, looking down. The chain had seared a fine line straight through the glove, and through the charred leather I could see a streak of red skin across her fingers.

"What were you thinking?" I demanded.

Roe glared at me and yanked her hand free. "What else could I have done?" she asked.

She was right, I figured, but it wasn't like I was going to tell her so, not when she'd hurt herself.

Allan glanced at her. "Thank you," he whispered.

Roe flashed a smile at him and nodded.

I pushed down a flare of jealousy. Roe always wanted to help people. That's why she'd joined up with me. That was it, I told myself as I turned away to find our first aid kit. That was all.

"So," I said to Allan as I bound up Roe's fingers. "What we just witnessed—"

He nodded. "That was Missy trying to force me to shift."

I frowned, doubly glad I'd shot him in the leg. If I said that out loud, though, Roe would scold me. So I settled for, "Tell us what really happened with the ring, then. If you're so anxious for us to believe your innocence."

Allan nodded and straightened up. "The part about giving the ring to my cousin was true. I didn't tell Missy. But it's not because we have any debt... she knew that. That's why she yelled at me after..." His voice trailed off, and he shook his head. "I knew she wouldn't buy it, but that at that point my hope was that you guys would, and you'd leave."

"Well, it sort of worked," I said.

"Yeah." He snorted. "Now I'm glad it only 'sort of'

worked, because if it had completely worked, I don't think we'd be having this chance to talk right now."

The guy was smart, I'd give him that.

"The truth is, I gave it to my cousin so I could get some cash Missy didn't know about. I figured if she noticed the missing ring, I'd tell her it must have fallen off at my job or something."

I raised an eyebrow. "So what was your plan to deal with the necklace?"

Allan shrugged. "I just wanted the cash ready for when I had a plan."

I knotted the bandage around Roe's hand and leaned back against my desk. "You know how we found that ring, right? It was near the bodies of three men at the docks...well, I should say, what remained of the bodies. They're gonna have a hard time if anyone hopes to identify the remains from what you left."

Allan's lips tightened. "I'm aware. Missy found out and confronted me last night. And then she..." He gestured to the necklace. "The next thing I knew, I woke up on the shoreline. Human. Covered in blood. Next to..." His voice choked off.

After a moment, he continued in a softer voice. "I had barely swum out into the water before I heard voices. A couple of guys with lanterns came down to the shore and saw the bodies, and...that's where you guys come in, I guess."

"Your cousin worked for Niall Byrne, the mob boss," I said shortly. "And Niall figured that Roe and I were the only ones he could bully into keeping quiet about it." I pulled my collar to one side, showing Allan my necklace once again.

His eyes widened, and he stood up abruptly, shoving his chair back. "You're not...you're..."

So he knew enough to know to realize what my new accessory was doin' to me. "Relax," I told him. "I ain't particularly fond of Niall either. We'll figure out a way to deal with this. Get Missy off your back, and Niall off ours." I turned to Roe. "Speaking of that... any ideas?"

Roe pulled her satchel closer and rummaged through it. "Have you tried anything, Allan?" she asked. "To try to break the necklace?"

"I took wire cutters to it once. Didn't leave a dent." Allan shrugged. "Like I said, my family was more concerned about fitting in with human society. I was never taught anything about our heritage, or anything about the Sidhé, for that matter. And I don't really know any Sidhé in the city. Missy made sure of that."

Roe frowned as she pulled a small wooden chest from the satchel and placed it on her desk. I sidled closer and craned my neck as she opened it. Despite never asking her about her curator training, I was curious.

Inside the box was a black cloth lining, dividing the

chest into various parts. A few twigs and some withered bark lay in one compartment, and various other bits and pieces lay in the others. I frowned.

"Is that..."

"Rowan. Yes." Roe glanced up at me, then looked away. "Can you get me the gloves from my coat pocket, please?"

I retrieved the gloves, her nicer leather pair, and handed them to her. Rowan. I glanced warily at the berries and bark and twigs in the compartment again. As a half-fae, I wasn't nearly as susceptible to any of this like she or Allan were... still, I didn't like the thought of Roe walking around with rowan in her pocket. That stuff could kill a fae... or drive them crazy. I'd heard tell that some of them treated it as a drug, like cocaine, taking hits of the stuff to enhance their speed and strength.

At the same time... I glanced at the desk drawer where I kept a thick rod of pure iron. As a half-fae, cold iron didn't bother me, but it could easily maim a full fae with a tap. Guess I shouldn't be blaming Roe. At least she had a reason to carry the stuff other than paranoia.

Roe lifted the top compartments from the chest, then used her gloved hand to remove a thin rod of iron. As she closed her fingers around it, I saw her hand twitch, as if losing some control over the muscles. She tightened her fingers.

"Roe." I put my hand on her arm. "Show me how to do it."

Roe glanced up at me, then nodded. She held out the rod.

I took it. The iron felt strange and heavy in my hand, but there was no burning sensation, no muscle weakness. I had the sense that too long of an exposure might result in some weakness, but as long as it wasn't rusty, it didn't spell a death sentence for me.

"Here's what we do," Roe said, half-turning to Allan. "If Owan can use this iron to scrape the ogham engraved into those links, then we should be able to snap the necklace."

Allan's shoulders hunched. "That's pure iron. I can feel it from here."

"You work in construction," I said irritably.

"I'm a carpenter," he snapped back. "As long as we don't use ash wood, I'm fine, but that doesn't mean I like it."

"What happens to kelpies if they're touched with iron, Allan?" Roe asked.

"I don't know. When I'm around it, I can feel it—it's like an itch at the back of my skull that I can't get rid of. But I've never touched the stuff just to find out." He tapped the necklace around his neck. "Silver's conductive to magic. That's why this works well to bind me. What happens when you hold iron to that?"

"Sparks, probably," Roe said. "Some discomfort. I don't

know. I've never really done this before."

"I thought you said you knew how to handle relics!"

"I'm training for that," Roe said snappishly. She rubbed between her eyes.

Allan suddenly stiffened again, and the necklace's chain started gently glowing. He twisted his head, trying to get away from the glowing bridle on his chest. "Let's get this done with," he hissed. "Before I shift, bullet or not."

I wasn't sure that's how it worked, but he was right—it was better to get this done. I grabbed the ruined pair of Roe's gloves from the desk, folding the gloves over themselves so they provided a double layer of protection from the hot metal. As I raised the chain from the back of Allan's neck and slipped the gloves under it, I saw a thin line of pink, raised scar tissue along the neckline of the shirt.

I slipped the iron rod under the chain, careful not to touch Allan's skin with it. As soon as the iron made contact with the silver, there was a sparking noise and the smell of hot metal. Allan yelped and twisted away from me. The movement yanked the chain in my hand, and for a split second I thought he would pull back.

Instead, the chain snapped, the middle of it coming apart in my hands like a piece of wet paper. I stepped back out of Allan's reach, my arm out in front of Roe. As if I could

protect her in this close space if this guy decided he wanted
to shred us.

Allan's hand went to the back of his neck, as if he
couldn't quite believe the necklace was gone. He bowed his
head, and his shoulders shook once, twice. I wasn't sure if he
was laughing or crying. Then he glanced over to me and
smiled. "Thank you."

After a moment too long of waiting, I said, "Don't
mention it."

Roe took the broken necklace from my hand and set it
aside. She picked up my first aid kit. "Well...let's get that
wound taken care of then."

After I'd dug the bullet out of Allan's leg and applied
salve and a bandage, he stood, testing his weight on the leg.
It held, though he looked a little shaky. He held his hand out
to me.

"Thank you, Mr. Craig," he said quietly. "I appreciate
the work you've done." He glanced at Roe, and the smile
became a grin. "You too, Miss Gillam."

"I wouldn't thank us just yet," Roe said. "You need to get
out of New York. Before Missy figures out where you are."

"Oh, trust me. I already know."

I spun around, taking two short, quick steps back to my
desk. Missy Dullahan stood in the doorway, a gun in her
hand. Somehow, she'd managed to open the door without any

of us hearing it. Her eyes blazed in fury as she glanced back and forth between us, then focused on Roe.

"I should've seen it," she spat. "You're like him, ain't you?" She jerked her head at Allan. "A monster."

Allan flinched. "Missy," he whispered.

Missy looked at him, her mouth pinched in worry. "Allan. Surely you can understand. I love you, but...I had to keep you in check."

"*What*?" Allan growled. His hands balled into fists.

"Once you told me what you were, I knew...I couldn't live without you, but I couldn't wait on pins and needles for the day you couldn't handle your inner nature anymore." Missy's eyes filled with tears. "I did this to protect you. To protect us."

I watched the gun in her hand. It never wavered.

"Missy," Roe said in her almost-Southern drawl that I loved so much. "I don't know who you think you're foolin', but it ain't us."

Missy's eyes snapped back to her, and her fingers tightened on the gun. "Like you'd know, you coldhearted *fae*."

Roe blinked in shock. I wondered if she'd ever had anyone use *fae* as an invective.

"That's enough, Missy." Allan took a step forward.

She jerked back. "I have iron bullets in here, Allan. So

don't you make me use them."

They stood glaring at each other for a moment, both tensed. I slowly moved my hand from my side to Roe's arm. The iron bullets might not bother Allan—iron for fae, silver for shifters, after all—but a stray bullet could sure as hell hurt Roe. Or me, if they were at all rusted.

The girl clearly didn't know what she was talkin' about. Not only did she get the metal wrong, but protecting her from Allan's 'inner nature'? That was beyond ridiculous. Sidhé had perfect control over themselves, unless someone else messed with their minds.

Which brought me to another point.

"Missy," I said. "Where the hell did you find someone to make that relic for you?"

Her eyes twitched over to me, then just as quickly went back to Allan. "I made it."

"That's bull," Roe said angrily. "You couldn't have made that. It takes years to learn how to make ogham and focus glamour into objects, and you're not even Sidhé. There's no possible way you could have made that."

"Like you know anything, fae," Missy spat.

"That's precisely why I would know, yes," Roe snapped. She stepped forward, between me and Allan and Missy.

Missy's gun swung to point at Roe's midsection. I nearly shouted, nearly yanked Roe back to my side, but instead I forced myself still and clenched my hands. One twitch of Missy's finger, and Roe would have an iron bullet in her.

Roe stuck her chin out. "I know because I'm fae. Have you ever heard of glamour? The curators?"

Missy frowned.

"I didn't think so. But you see, Missy . . ." Roe's tone changed. Softer, calmer, lower. "I know about all of those things. And I can help you." She was inching closer to Missy as she spoke. "Just tell me about the relic, Missy. Where did you get it? Who gave it to you?"

"I . . ." Missy licked her lips. "I p-promised I wouldn't. I paid a lot of money for that. I . . ."

"Missy, c'mon, can't you just see that—" Allan took a step forward and crumpled, catching himself against the wall with a grunt of pain.

Missy started and looked at him. "Allan!" Her voice was panicked.

I lunged forward and snatched at her hand. The gun roared, and heat scorched along my wrist. I twisted Missy's arm, and the gun clunked to the ground. I found it with my foot and kicked it away. In just a few seconds I had Missy's arms pinned.

Missy looked over at Allan, her dark eyes wide and frightened. "Don't let them hurt me!"

"They're not going to." Allan sat down, his hand pressed

against the wound on his leg. Pain and tiredness etched lines into his face. "What do we do now?"

"Take her to the police station and press charges," I said.

"But how—"

"We can come up with something. If she tries to tell them the truth, she'll sound like she's crazy." I shrugged one shoulder. "And even if they let her go, it will buy you time."

"Time?" Missy demanded. "Time for what?"

Allan ignored her and looked up at me, nodding. "Let's do that then."

The four of us trekked down to the nearest police station, where we turned Missy into the authorities, telling them Allan had come to us about a missing piece of jewelry and his wife had followed us, then held everyone at gunpoint. Missy sullenly refused to say anything. It took time, but eventually the police thanked us, and we left the station.

The moon hung overhead, pale and blurred by thin wisps of clouds. I stuck my hands in my pockets and glanced over at Allan. "What do you think you'll do now?"

He shrugged. "Move far away from here. Find some more construction work." His eyes darkened, and he glanced away, towards the bay. "You—you guys said I killed people. What's going to happen with that?"

I rubbed the bridle necklace in my pocket between my

thumb and forefinger. Niall would be furious if we let Allan go, but I wasn't about to turn him in when it would certainly spell his death. "You just get outta town," I said. "We'll figure out something."

Allan nodded gratefully and all but ran down the street, soon disappearing from sight.

Roe looked over at me and raised one eyebrow. "You already have a plan, don't you?"

"I have a half-baked idea that may or may not work."

Roe stepped to my side and put one hand on my arm. "Better to get it over with?"

With my free hand, I reached up and touched the chain around my neck. It was definitely tighter than it had been, and I could feel it cutting into my skin. Soon—very, very soon—it would get too tight to breathe.

"Yeah," I said wearily. "Better to get it over with."

WE didn't have any trouble gaining entry when we knocked on the warehouse. The trouble came when we told Niall we wouldn't tell him the name of the guy who had killed his men.

The Unseelie's face was deathly still, but his eyes narrowed just a touch. "I see," he said coldly. "You must know I consider this a breach of our agreement, Mr. Craig."

I stepped forward, keeping my hands in the pockets of

my loose coat. I could feel Roe's eyes on my back, waiting for a signal for me. The trouble was that the four men in Niall's office were also waiting for a signal from me. We'd already been relieved of our guns, but I was pretty sure they had theirs.

The image of Roe floating away in dark waters flashed in my mind. I steeled my resolve and stepped closer to Niall. I had one chance at this.

"I don't really consider something made under duress an 'agreement'," I said shortly.

Niall shrugged one shoulder. "It doesn't really matter what you call it, does it, now, Owan? Relics aren't precisely caring about how they kill, if that is their purpose." He started to turn away from me, one hand coming from his suit pocket to gesture.

I sprang the remaining distance and seized his wrist with one hand, using my other hand to wrap a chain around it.

Niall froze and looked down. The silver glitter of the bridle necklace glistened, almost but not quite around his wrist, just my thumb keeping the links of the chain from closing to one another.

"Oh, don't I know it," I said softly.

Niall glared at me and spoke in an equally soft voice. "What is this? Some trinket you picked up on your adventures?"

"Not quite." I smiled. "It happens to belong to the victim of a fairly powerful witch. Someone who, I imagine, would love to know who set us on her trail." Maybe I was stretching the truth there a bit, but Niall didn't need to know that. "Once I set these links together—" I pressed my thumb into Niall's wrist— "the necklace will fuse together, and she'll be able to tell where you are."

Niall looked down at the bracelet again, then raised his eyes to mine. He tipped his chin just slightly. "Well then."

"Boss?" one of the men asked.

"Stand down," Niall snapped. He raised his hand and spoke a word in Gaelic.

The tight torc around my neck suddenly loosened. I resisted the urge to gasp in a deep breath and watched as the torc rolled off my shoulder and into Niall's outstretched hand, where it coiled like a snake.

He carefully placed it on his desk. "Fair's fair, Mr. Craig."

"Yeah, but see, now I need some insurance to make sure your boys don't blow me full of holes."

"Ah, yes." Niall smiled tightly. "Let me walk you and your lovely associate to the door, shall I?"

Niall and I began our awkward walk to the door. I felt Roe clutch my other sleeve, sticking close to me so that I almost felt claustrophobic with Niall on one side and her on the other.

The goons followed, all of them looking irritated but knowing they couldn't do anything about their boss's stand-down order.

I dragged Niall a few steps from the warehouse door, just to be safe, then turned to him and hissed, "I hope you don't take this the wrong way, but I'd rather not be dragged out of my office in the middle of the night by your guys again."

Niall's grin was sharp. "Fine with me. Pleasure doing business with you, Mr. Craig."

"Wish I could say the same." I let go of his wrist.

Niall stepped back towards his goons, and Roe and I beat it out of there as quickly as we could. I looked back, several times, but didn't see anyone following us.

After a time, I caught Roe's hand and pulled her to the side. We made our way down to the shoreside and stood for a moment, staring across the bay at the lights of Brooklyn wavering in the black water.

I pulled the bridle necklace out of my pocket and stared down at it, the tiny silver chain twinkling in the orange glow of the city.

I wanted to drop the damn thing into the water, let it sink to the bottom of the bay. Such magic shouldn't exist.

I glanced over at Roe. "Think your people would be

interested in looking at this?"

She bit her lower lip. "I think it would be best. If there's someone out there creating *new* relics . . ." Her voice trailed away.

She didn't have to finish. It was obvious. Up till now, we only ever had to worry about old relics. Things made back when the paths were open between our world and the fae world, Tir Ni-all. Those paths had been hidden a long time ago, and since then, relics had become more and more rare...less and less powerful. Just like fae glamour, they faded with time, with their connection to Tir Ni-all cut off.

But if someone out there had found ways to make new relics, that was a whole new mess of trouble.

Roe held her hand out. I poured the chain into her cupped palm, then placed my hand over hers.

"Keep it safe," I said quietly.

"You know you can trust me, Owan."

"I know I can, sweetheart." I smiled at her. "I know I can."

THE GREEN MAN

I swear, I know it sounds like these stories always start when it's raining or in the dark dead of night, but that's just the business we're in. Bad things happen at night—bad things and fae things.

Seein' as how I'm the one and only half-fae private detective in all of New York City, it's kinda fitting that I'm the one gettin' stuck with all of this.

Roe and I were walking home after seeing an off-Broadway Shakespearean play, the one about the fairies. Shakespeare was never my thing—took too many liberties with his source material as far as I was concerned—but at least it had been amusin'.

"Think I'd be the bee's knees with a donkey head, Roe?" I asked, dodging around a puddle on the sidewalk.

Roe grinned at me from under her umbrella. She'd been the smart one and actually brought an umbrella—all I had was my hat and coat to protect me from the drizzle.

"I figure there's no need for you to go advertisin' what you are. Might make clients scarce."

I laughed and moved closer to her, letting her umbrella cut some of the rain. "We're out of the office, Miss Gillam. We don't talk business."

"All right, Mr. Craig. What do you suggest we talk about?"

I couldn't see her face anymore, but her tone suggested she was grinning.

See, that's what I liked about Roe. She was funny, easy-going, and smart as a whip. It's why I hired her, and not as a secretary, but as a full-fledged partner. Her bein' full fae and easy on the eyes was just a side benefit, but I didn't tell her that.

Wind whistled down the street, blowing my coat and blasting chilly rain right into my face. I squinted and ducked behind Roe's umbrella until the wind died down, hearing Roe laugh at me.

Then I heard a new sound—the sound of breaking glass.

The tap-tap of Roe's shoes on the pavement stopped, and she reached back for my arm. "Did you hear that?"

"Yeah." I glanced around the street. The pouring rain made halos around the streetlights, but despite this glow, the street remained dim, shadows overpowering the sidewalks close to the buildings. I unbuttoned my coat with my free hand and reached inside, unsnapping the underarm holster keeping my gun in place.

Was it gauche to admit to wearing a gun to the theater? Probably.

A deeper shadow moved among the shadows across the street from us. I glanced at Roe as she carefully lowered her umbrella. Rain dripped from her hat as she reached into her coat pocket.

We darted around a streetlight and kept in the darker middle of the street as we approached. The sounds seemed to be coming from a store on the corner of the avenue. Thankfully, if we were careful, the rain muffled our footsteps.

Glass glinted on the sidewalk. The exterior of the shop was painted black, the gold-lettered sign above the broken window proclaiming it to be Hartford & Sons, a jewelry store.

I glanced past the broken chunks of glass left in the window. I could just hear the sounds of glass grinding underfoot. Someone was moving around in there, in the pitch dark.

Just as I thought that, a light flared. I pulled back, but soon realized that the light was being blocked by someone— some*thing*. It was huge, human-shaped, but moving in a strange, jerky motion. A troll? Would a troll drop their glamoured human form while robbing a jewelry store?

I glanced over at Roe again. She frowned. Glass crunched again, and when I looked back, I saw it had smashed open a jewelry case.

"What is that?" Roe whispered.

"Dunno," I muttered.

The interior of the shop went quiet, and the figure stopped moving in the dim light. The pattering of the rain was the only sound. I reached back, found Roe's shoulder, and gently pushed her back away from the window, around the corner of the shop. I pressed my back to the brick and held my breath.

Glass cracked, and suddenly long, spindly fingers wrapped around the corner of the building. Those fingers didn't look humanoid—they were too long, too thin, and had far too many joints that looked like knots in a plank of wood. In fact, I was pretty sure they were long enough that they could have easily wrapped around my chest. The shadow of a head appeared against the streetlight outside—as large as my upper half, though I couldn't see much more since it was only a silhouette.

Roe's fingers dug into my arm.

We waited for another agonizing few seconds as the thing stared out of the shop window. Then it tapped its fingers on the brick and withdrew. More sounds of shattering glass came from the shop. I relaxed my grip on my gun.

Roe's lips tickled my ear. "It's a golem."

"A wooden golem?" I whispered back.

I felt more than saw her shrug. Well, maybe it was possible. She was the one doing the curator training, after all. I wondered what signs she'd spotted in the brief glimpse we'd had of the creature.

The sharp blast of a cop's whistle cut through the night air. "You there! What do you think you're doin'?"

More glass smashed, and I had a split second to flatten myself back against the wall as the huge, dark shape of the golem came barrelling around the corner. My heart leapt to my throat, but it seemed to not even notice us as it fled.

I tugged on Roe's hand, taking off after the golem. I had no desire for some nosy cop to decide that I need to be detained for questioning—and I didn't want to lose sight of it.

Street lights flickered as the golem ran past it, just enough that I never got a full, good look at it. From what I could see, the golem's skin was cracked and textured like bark. Its joints creaked like old branches in a strong wind as it ran. It looked back over its shoulder, and I got the impression of a smooth, flat face with no features save for eye sockets, burning with a tiny pinprick of glowing light deep within them.

It suddenly veered to the right, down another alley. I darted after it.

Something heavy smashed into my face. It was like someone had snatched my feet out from under me—I landed flat on my back, stars whirling in my vision.

"Back off!" Roe shouted from somewhere behind me. "I'm serious! Back away!"

The golem snarled above me, sending cold prickles of fear along my body. Then a pressure released from my leg— a pressure that felt an awful lot like thin, spindly fingers— and the creaking footsteps vanished into the distance.

I swore, blinked, shook my head—and swore again as the motion made my temples feel like they were about to burst.

Roe knelt beside me, gripping my arm. "Are you all right?"

"That was a mistake." I pushed against the ground with one hand, but let Roe pull most of my weight until I was upright. Warm blood pulsed from my nose, dripping onto my chin and coat. It mixed with the cold rainwater on my face, creating a lukewarm, slimy texture and a wish for a good, hot shower.

"What was a mistake? Careening around the corner, or chasing the golem in the first place?"

"None of your sass."

Roe grinned at me. "You can take it out of my pay later, boss."

I rolled my eyes at her and turned, feeling my way along the brick wall. I still felt incredibly unsteady on my feet.

"Where do you think you're goin'?" Roe demanded.

"We need to get back to the crime scene and see—"

"He must have clocked you harder than I thought." Roe tugged on my sleeve, pulling me to a halt. "We are not going back to the crime scene. Not with you looking like you were in a street brawl. You know you won't get anywhere with the cops when you look like that."

True enough. Besides that, the agony in my head wasn't dying... instead, it was spreading along my forehead and looked to be turning into a whale of a headache.

"Fine," I muttered. "Fine. Let's go home, I guess."

I staggered back to my apartment, leaning on Roe's shoulder. The icy rain felt good on my throbbing head. We made it up to my room without any trouble—miraculously, since I had Brooklyn's nosiest landlady who possessed the ears of a cat sidhé. I'd wanted to take the fire escape, but Roe had overruled me, and by that time I couldn't exactly move much without her help.

Roe set me down at my kitchen table and crossed to the cabinets. By this time, she knew exactly where my medical kit was.

"So, what was that thing?" I asked.

She tossed me a kitchen towel. "A wooden golem."

I blinked and folded the towel, pressing it tightly against my nose. "I thought they made golems out of clay."

"In Jewish kabbalistic tradition, yes. They're clay men brought to life by scrolls put into their mouths."

"Now you're just showing off."

Roe shrugged. "Perhaps there's a better word for this type of creature in Sidhé tradition, but for the moment, 'golem' will suffice." She came back, setting the medical kit on the table in front of us, and sat down in the other chair. "I managed to get a good look at it while you were...distracting it."

"Getting pummeled within an inch of my life, you mean."

"Big baby."

I grunted and rifled through the bag for a piece of gauze, then pressed it to my nose.

"This golem was made from wood, like I said earlier. Not clay—living, green wood, with leaves still on the branches and dirt still clinging to the roots."

"Someone made a tree uproot itself and then turned it into a golem?"

She shrugged.

I grumbled under my breath. Not only did my entire face feel like I'd been run over by a truck, but the power it would take to uproot a tree and turn it into a moving, living thing with SOME kind of thought process...well, it sounded like powerful glamour to me. And I just LOVED cases with powerful glamour users in the mix. It also tickled something in the back of my brain, but when I tried to chase it down, the thought disappeared quicker than a pregnant singer in a jazz club.

"Either way, what can we do about it?" I asked Roe. "How do you stop something like that, short of settin' it on fire?"

Roe winced.

"Yeah, that's my thought as well." Setting it on fire wasn't an option that thrilled me. Fire and glamour tended to explosively protest their forced proximity. Not to mention I'd seen fire give glamour users magical backlash that landed them in the hospital. It wasn't a good combination.

Roe tapped her lower lip with a finger as she stared out the kitchen window. I leaned back in my chair, content to watch her think for a moment as my mind wandered--and, inevitably, it ended up where it usually did, thinkin' about Roe's hair and how soft the curls looked, and the way her eyes sparkled with life and curiosity.

The first time I'd met Roe, I'd had the thought that she

had the type of hair a guy would like to run his fingers through. It was time to admit it—I was that guy. Give me a girl with soft curls and a sharp wit, and I'd take her over a stable full of dames with great gams and curves any day of the week. Roe was a lovely lass, sure, and that made her even more attractive...

"Owan?"

I started. Roe was staring back at me with a puzzled look. I shut my mouth and sat up straight. "Sorry. Must've drifted off there for a bit." I grinned. "I wasn't starin' anywhere inappropriate, was I?"

Roe let out a soft huff of laughter and rolled her eyes. "You feelin' okay?"

"Oh, yeah, fine." I gestured with the bloody gauze. "Never better."

Roe checked her watch, a gesture that made me turn to look at the clock sitting on the bookshelf across the room. I winced. Nearly midnight.

"Tell me honestly." Roe had a sharp look in her blue eyes. "Do you think you have a concussion? Should I stay here tonight, or will you be all right on your own?"

I held my finger up in front of my face, moving it back and forth. My vision felt smooth, and when I gently probed at the back of my neck, I couldn't detect any stiffness. It was on the tip of my tongue to ask her to stay, but I stopped myself. I wasn't confident we could sneak past my landlady again, and the last thing I wanted was to compromise Roe's reputation to those who cared about such things. "It's a flat-out miracle, but I think I'm all right."

"All right, well—" Roe stood, gathering her umbrella and purse from where she'd dropped them on the counter. "I suppose we should pick this discussion back up in the morning, then. Maybe we'll have clearer heads."

"I hope I'd have a clearer one, anyway." I wadded up the gauze and pitched it towards the sink. I'd clean up tomorrow. "I don't expect you to come in until eight or nine, all right?"

"Only if you do the same."

I grinned. "You're going to bully me into taking care of myself, aren't you?"

"Someone has to." Roe smiled and pointed to the window over the fire escape. "I'll let myself out, shall I?"

As she raised the window, I stood, feeling jittery. "Careful, eh, doll?" I tried to pass my concern off with a small laugh.

She turned a sharp grin toward me as she stepped out onto the metal lattice. "Sure will, boss. Now go to bed." She unfurled the umbrella and started making her way down the slick stairs.

I waited just long enough to make sure she was safely at the bottom of the steps and heading down the street before I

went into my bedroom, collapsing on the bed without even
bothering to undress.

THE next morning, we met at the little diner close to the
office, as had become our custom over the last few months.
I'd chosen it because it had decent food for the price, the
coffee was hot and strong, and----it was a favorite of the beat
cops in the area. This morning, we were a little later than
usual, but it gratified me to still see several blue uniforms as I
walked in the door.

Roe and I sat at the diner as we ate, occasionally talking
to each other as we looked over the various sheets of the
morning paper, that other patrons had helpfully left, for
potential work leads. But mostly, we were listening—while
pretending to not listen—to the racket the cops made as the
night shift got dinner before heading home and the morning
shift got breakfast before heading out on the streets.

Apparently the city had been active last night—there
was talk of several shootings, including one that everyone
agreed was self-defense on the dame's part, one or two hold-
ups, some gang violence, and one smuggling bust down at
the riverfront. I exchanged a look with Roe. She shrugged.
No need to exchange words with this one—we both were
thinking of the same mob, run by a fae named Niall Byrne.
We both had a personal beef with the guy, given he'd once

kidnapped me, and then later had coerced me and Roe into trying to hunt down a kelpie that had killed some of his men. Hadn't heard much from him lately—my sincere hope was that at least a couple of our anonymous tips to the police were finally panning out and they were keeping him pinned down. Or that he was keeping the promise I'd extracted last time, that he would no longer bother us. Either option was good with me--I had no truck with the mob, and I damn well wanted Roe away from them too. I hadn't cared for the way Byrne had looked at her when he'd discovered she was training to be a curator.

Roe tapped my arm. When I glanced at her, she nodded down the counter to a couple of beat cops, their uniforms looking rumpled and damp from the rain. I sipped my coffee and tilted my head in their direction, trying to pick up their words in the chatter of the crowded diner.

See, that's where the nice thing about being half-fae comes in. It has its disadvantages—plenty of 'em, like the danger of getting poisoned by rusty iron—but it has its perks, especially for this business.

One of the cops took a long draw from his coffee cup and set it back on the counter with a clatter. "It's the weirdest thing. All this smashed up glass, and cases of the good stuff caved in—looked like a giant had stepped on it. But none of it was taken, not a single bit of it. The owner said most of the stuff taken was gold plate and glass—the bits that look all sparkly but ain't worth much. Junk no fence would pay much for."

"So whoever took it, they weren't no expert." The second cop dragged his hand over his face. He looked like he was downing a pot of coffee just to drag himself home. He took a gulp, then gestured to his buddy. "Go on."

"Right, they sure ain't no expert. So tracking down whoever did this will be a tough job. Chances are he's workin' on his own, which means we probably won't find any leads with our usual suspects, if ya catch my drift. Poor Detective O'Rourke's gotta be pulling out his hair over this one."

"Yeah, well, the Irish Bulldog's gotta be the perfect guy for the job. He'll run the thief to ground." The second cop threw back his head, noisily chugging one last cup of coffee, before putting his cup down. The waitress gave him an annoyed look as the coffee dregs splashed out of the cup, but he was apparently too tired to notice. He stood up, dropping some change on the counter. "I'm off. See ya tomorrow night."

The talkative cop waved him away, then sat drinking another cup more slowly than before. Despite the enormous amount of caffeine he'd downed, now that he no longer had an audience, he looked tired and droopy. I'd place a bet that he'd end up face down on the counter, snoring, if he didn't start home in the next few minutes.

I scraped up the last of my over-easy eggs with a triangle of toast, considering. I was on pretty good terms with most of the local constabulary. I'd even been a cop once, though it hadn't stuck for too long before I'd struck out on my own. It was hard to deal with cases involving the Sidhé when you had supervisors breathin' down your neck and demanding why you didn't follow protocol or another. None of my superiors would've accepted, "Sorry sir, but the only way to stop that berserking troll was iron bullets and I just didn't have any of those in my pockets, so I had to stab him with a piece of rebar I'd snitched from a construction site", as an excuse.

Heh, one of these days I had to tell Roe that story. It'd been before she came to work for me, right near the beginning of my career as a private investigator, and I was pretty sure she'd find it amusing.

I'd never been stationed with O'Rourke, but I knew of him. The moniker 'Irish Bulldog' fit him well, if the stories were true. The guy wouldn't let a thing go once he had hold of it. He'd fought his way up from the multitudes of Irish beat cops to become detective, about the same time I was leaving the force.

"What're you grinning about?" Roe asked.

I finished the last bite of my egg and toast. "You done?"

Roe pointed to her empty plate. "Have been for a while." She rustled the newspaper page she was holding, folding it back along the crease. "So—are we gonna find something else to do today, or are we gonna stick our noses into that case?"

I pulled change from my wallet and placed it on the counter, enough to cover both our breakfasts plus tip. "C'mon. I think it's time you meet some of our boys in blue."

As we walked, I relayed all that I remembered about O'Rourke to Roe.

"How careful do we have to be of him?" she asked.

I shrugged. It was a good question, one that was always in the back of anyone's mind if they were a being with any Sidhé blood in them. You never knew who might see through the glamour, who had the second sight—and how they would react, even if it wasn't a surprise to them. Some people had been taught properly, but they were few nowadays, especially in America, and even more especially in a big city, where life was already far too busy for superstition to take hold.

Even at this hour of the morning, the street in front of the jewelry shop was filled with vehicles. Several police radio cars, a nice sedan I guessed belonged to the owner, and one or two others—maybe reporters? Several bluebacks milled about the place still, looking reluctant to leave even though the detective had already arrived.

Detective O'Rourke—a tall, lank man quite the opposite of the stereotypical Irish cop--stood off to the side, talking to a shorter Jewish guy with corkscrew curls sticking up everywhere on his head that wasn't covered with a kippah. Every now and then, O'Rourke would nod and jot something in a notebook, but for the most part, his eyes stayed fixed on the shop owner.

Almost as if he did indeed have the second sight, or at least some weird sixth sense, O'Rourke turned around and made eye contact with me as we approached. His gray-brown eyes glanced curiously at Roe for a moment. Then he snapped his notebook shut and slipped it into the pocket of his suit coat.

"Thank you, Mr. Levy, that'll be all." Despite being born and bred in the United States, O'Rourke still had a bit of an Irish burr clinging to his words. He wove his way around a cluster of cops and stretched his hand out to me, the smile on his face friendly.

Well, that took a load off my mind, at least.

Although, by the gesture, he was also effectively blocking us from the crime scene.

"Owan Craig, I presume," he said, then chuckled at his own joke.

"O'Rourke." I shook. "Word must get around. We

haven't met in person and I'm just forgetting it, right?"

"Nah, nah, but as ya said, word gets around about the private eye who keeps his ear to the ground and knows what's what."

I eyed him. Those beady blue eyes showed nothing but innocence, but humans were good liars. Especially cops. I motioned toward Roe. "O'Rourke, this is my assistant, Roe Gillam. Roe, Detective O'Rourke."

They shook hands, and I saw a faint raising of one of O'Rourke's eyebrows as he appraised Roe. "Assistant? Not 'secretary', eh?"

"No thanks," Roe said, still smiling despite the comment. "No sitting behind a desk all day for this girl."

He chuckled. "Sounds like you're a right bearcat and no mistake. Gotcher licenses?"

We dug into our pockets and produced them.

O'Rourke nodded. "That's all right, then. I don't mind letting you two have a sniff around, but..." He gave me a grin that only faintly disguised a stony stare. "You're not gonna cut me outta this, are you?"

"Absolutely not," I assured him.

"How did you two hear about this, if you don't mind me asking?"

I resisted the urge to glance over at Roe. It was better,

for now, if O'Rourke didn't know we'd been on the scene of the crime and witnessed it happening last night.

"Heard two beat cops talkin' about it in the dinner over breakfast," Roe volunteered before I could. "We don't have anything urgent today, so we thought we'd come over here and take a look for ourselves."

O'Rourke nodded again. "Well, sounds like you've got a fine set of ears on you, Miss Gillam." He chuckled and winked to let us know he meant it as a joke.

I smiled, although I didn't mean it. He was at least treating Roe politely, but the faint condescension in his tone was gettin' to me. Roe was handlin' it like a champ, though. "So, should we scram, or do you mind us hanging out here for a bit?"

"No, no, that's fine. I don't mind lettin' you know, we're a bit stumped on this one. Of course, it's only the first break-in of its kind. Might not even be a repeat incident anywhere else, but we'd like to get to the bottom of it as soon as possible." O'Rourke turned back to the crime scene and motioned for us to follow.

I glanced at Roe. First of its kind? It almost sounded like they were expecting more, the way he'd worded it. Roe shrugged and followed the detective into the smashed shop.

We spent about twenty minutes going over the details of the scene, but didn't find too much more than what we'd already gotten out of the cops at the diner. Several cops worked to sift jewelry and loose stones out of the smashed display cases. Glass crunched under our feet as we walked around, although there were slick patches of half-dried clay on the floor that seemed to puzzle the cops to no end.

"Our cats had messy boots, that's for sure," O'Rourke commented. "Most of these guys are more careful than that. Unfortunately, nothing's solid enough that we could try to take sole impressions."

"Cats, plural?" Roe asked.

"Yeah, I don't think one guy could create this much mess. It was storming last night, but smashing everything up like this would have been loud, drawing attention. Had to be several people workin' together. 'Sides, the beat cop who first spotted the intruders said there were at least three or four people who fled the scene." O'Rourke prodded at a puddle of clay and water with the toe of one shoe. "The whole gang must've gone to Central Park and rolled in a mud puddle first, though."

I crouched down and crumbled some of the damp clay between my fingers. This felt more like sticky bank mud to me, and I said so. "You plannin' on getting it analyzed?"

O'Rourke snorted. "I can just imagine the boys at the lab will love this, but yes. I'll take any needle I can find in this haystack."

"Do you think there will be more break-ins?" Roe asked.

O'Rourke leaned a little closer to her. "We haven't exactly announced it to the press, so keep this under wraps. But there's been a rash of break-ins at jewelry stores over the last couple of months. Nothin' quite like this—those jobs were a lot cleaner, and they actually took the good stuff. But I wouldn't be surprised to find that this is a copycat, or an offshoot of the same gang who don't know what they're doing."

Roe nodded. "Is there anything specific we can do to help you?"

O'Rourke shrugged. "You guys probably have connections I don't. Just keep your eyes open." He grinned at Roe. "And maybe keep those pretty ears to the ground."

I laughed. "You tryin' to put us on the informants' payroll, O'Rourke?"

He guffawed. "Maybe, maybe."

After a few more minutes of chitchat, we parted ways.

As soon as we were out of earshot, Roe said, "Do you think he knows what I am? Or you? He made cracks about both of our ears."

I nodded. That had bothered me, too, although I hadn't considered it from the angle she was worried over. As a full fae, Roe's ears were pointed. Sometimes she kept them hidden with her hair, but today, she'd styled her hair in an updo that left them exposed. A full-blooded fae like her had glamour—unlike me—but if O'Rourke had the second sight... "Hard to tell—the man plays things close to the vest. It's good to know he doesn't mind us pokin' around, though."

Roe's eyes twinkled. "Would his disapproval have stopped us?"

"'Course not. But it's nice to know there's a blueback who'd put in a good word for us if we're caught doin' things that might be a mite unethical."

"So... what now?"

"Now, we beat feet. Like O'Rourke said, the cat who snagged those goods can't know his way around the business too well. So we'll talk to a few folks. See a few friends about anyone tryin' to pass off cheap stuff, or if they've heard about a new guy in the game." I shook my sleeve back, checking my watch. "Better check up at the office first, though, just in case."

It didn't take us long to get back to the office, and it was a good thing we'd decided to pop in for a minute. As we walked into the building, the super—who kept a little office space right inside the front door—waved us over to his open doorway.

"Hey, Mr. Nowak," I said. "What's news?"

"There's a gal up waitin' for ya in your office." Nowak, an older Polish gentleman, squinted up at me with his one good eye. The man's scrunched-up face sometimes made me question whether he might have some Sidhé blood in his ancestry—cat Sidhé, or goblin perhaps. It wasn't unheard of.

I tried not to wince. The man was only doing us a favor, but who knew who the dame was. I didn't keep anything valuable in the office, but Roe had her curator's kit tucked in a bottom drawer of her desk, and I didn't like the thought of anyone having a chance to poke around. "How long ago?"

"Ten-fifteen minutes." The man shrugged. "Ain't seen her come back down, though."

I tipped him a few quarters in thanks and booked it for the elevators, muttering to Roe, "Let's hope she's a genuine client and not some kind of snoop."

Roe, I noticed, had tucked her hand into her inner jacket pocket, where I knew she kept her little revolver. I waited until the elevator door closed, then unbuttoned my coat and unsnapped my underarm holster.

We rode up to the office in silence and approached the door as quietly as we could. I didn't slam the door open, but I whipped it open pretty quick, startling the girl sitting in the waiting area.

I stopped. It was no wonder Mr. Nowak had noticed her, even if she hadn't spoken to him. It would've been hard to *not* notice this girl. She looked like she could be on the silver screen, not sittin' in our dingy office space in a demure gray suit, her gams crossed to show them off to their best advantage. Her hair was a perfect golden, falling in soft shimmering curls to her shoulders, and her pouty lips were painted a glossy shade of rose petal pink.

I knew *exactly* what she was doing, and it still caught me off guard enough that I stopped in the middle of the doorway.

Roe shouldered past me, giving me a raised eyebrow before smiling at the woman. "Hello! Sorry for your wait."

The woman stood, extending her hand to Roe. "No trouble." Her voice was low and throaty, tinged with a Jersey accent. She shuffled her feet back and forth, looking suddenly awkward.

I snapped myself out of my stupor and smiled reassuringly at her. "Yes, we apologize. This is Roe Gillam, and I'm Owan Craig." I shut the door and gestured her back to her seat. "What can we help you with, Miss...?"

"Gladys. Gladys Connor."

I crossed to my desk, leaning on it as Miss Connor took her seat again. Roe sat down behind her own desk, grabbing a notepad and pen. I watched her out of the corner of my eye, wondering what she thought of our prospective client. Roe caught me watching and offered a smile that had the barest hint of a biting smirk at the corners of her mouth. I couldn't tell if she was mocking me, or if there was something she found amusing about Miss Connor.

Miss Connor twisted her gloves together in her hands.

She still looked stunning, but the gesture made her seem much younger, almost childish.

"Would you like some coffee, miss?" I asked.

"Oh. Umm, no, no, I couldn't possibly be a bother." Miss Connor glanced between me and Roe.

"No trouble," Roe said, putting the notepad back down and standing again. She crossed the room to the hotplate and coffee percolator we had perched on a cupboard by the door. "You want any, Owan?"

I nearly raised an eyebrow at that. Roe and I were never formal with each other, but she tended to call me 'boss' or 'Mr. Craig' around others. Was Miss Connor making her jealous? I dismissed the thought immediately. Roe wasn't the jealous type. But something about this woman had gotten her back up. Best to proceed carefully. "While she's making the coffee, Miss Connor, would you mind tellin' me what brought you here today?" I reached over to Roe's desk and retrieved the notepad and pen, steadying it on one knee as I waited.

Miss Connor bit her lower lip, twisting her gloves together harder. If she didn't quit that, those gloves would be unwearable. "You can call me Gladys, Mr. Craig, that would be perfectly fine. I—" She hesitated, and once again I was struck by how young she seemed. She had the body and face of a confident, full-grown woman, but her nervous air reminded me of a kid trying to act like an adult.

"I—well, I've heard a bit about you, Mr. Craig, and you, Miss Gillam. So I thought—well, that you two might be best for this job." She took a deep breath. "I'm here about my brother. I'm his sole guardian—he's ten. We're twelve years apart. Our parents passed away a couple of years ago, and, well... Nick—that's my brother—he's had a rough time since then, especially since I've been trying to work and keep us both going. About a week ago, he..." Gladys looked down at her lap, biting her lower lip again. "He ran away, Mr. Craig."

I glanced up, meeting Roe's eyes over Gladys's bowed head. If the girl was acting, she was doing a fine job. Roe slightly lifted one shoulder—she didn't quite know what to make of this girl either, it seemed. But she still seemed hesitant, and I understood. Something was off about this girl, and her story seemed designed to tug at soft heartstrings.

Gladys looked up at me, her big baby blues soft and plaintive, half-filled with tears. Dammit, she was pouring it on thick.

Or, a voice in the back of my head murmured, *she's telling the truth.*

"So I guess you want me to find this kid brother of

yours?" I said.

She nodded.

"Can I ask a quick question?" Roe asked, stepping up to Gladys's side and placing a hand on her shoulder. "Why haven't you gone to the police, Gladys?"

"I have," Gladys answered softly. "I went to them that first evening, when Nick wasn't home for dinner. He might act like he hates me some days, but he never misses meals. He's growin' so much..." She dabbed a handkerchief to her eyes, pulling in a deep breath. "I went to them again the next day. But I don't think the police really care about one little kid in this big city."

I struggled to keep from wincing. My experience was that there were plenty of officers who cared—but like she said, her brother was a little kid in a big city, and the cops had limited resources. I jotted down a note to check in with the guys I still knew on the force. "Okay. Tell me about your brother—where did he go to school? Who were his friends? Role models? Did he have any special hobbies, like train watching or baseball?"

As Gladys filled me in, Roe silently served out three cups of strong black coffee. As I took mine, I realized it was only about half-filled with coffee, and that Roe had used the liquid to paste a small piece of paper on the inside of the cup, out of Gladys's sight.

Glamoured jewelry.

My stomach knotted at those words.

Gladys was still talking about her brother, which made me glad, because it meant she hadn't noticed me freeze, even if it wasn't for long. I set my cup of coffee aside and glanced up at Roe, nodding to let her know I'd seen her message.

As was the way with glamour, now that I knew it was there, things became plain. Gladys was still tall, but with more of the air of a coltish lankiness than a full-grown woman. The nervous gestures I'd noticed that made her seem younger fit her true age—I guessed her to be sixteen or seventeen. Maybe, in a few years, she'd actually be that silver screen beauty, but not now. What was more, as Gladys paused in her story, I noticed the faint point to the tips of her ears and the subtle way her eyes shifted from sky-blue to storm cloud gray.

Great. So Gladys was also half-fae. Why the hell she hadn't said so was beyond me—most in the community knew that I was a half-fae and that my assistant was full fae.

"That should do it, right, Owan?" Roe's tone was pointed, and I realized she was answering a question Gladys had asked. She nodded at me.

"Yeah, I think that's all the information we need."

Gladys glanced between us. "You think you'll be able to find Nick?"

"I don't want to promise anything," Roe said gently. "It's a big city. But we'll do our best."

As she ushered the girl out of the office, I slapped my notebook down on my desk and leaned back on my hands, frowning. Where would she have gotten her hands on glamoured jewelry? There was a disturbing amount of glamoured items going around lately... I thought of our last case, a kelpie controlled by his non-Sidhé spouse, via a glamoured necklace. As far as I'd known, the curators had had the illegal trade in relics well in hand since around the turn of the century.

Roe came back into the office, quickly crossing the room to grab her coat off the back of her chair.

"Where are you going?" I asked, straightening up.

"I'm going to follow her." Roe gave me a worried glance. "Those earrings... Owan..." She shook her head and swung her coat over her arms.

"Whoa—hold up a second!" I ran after her. "Is that smart?"

"Maybe not, but I'm tired of relics running around the city under the curators' noses and not knowing where they're from."

"You really think that girl could tell you?"

"I don't know what to think, Owan." Roe straightened her hat and sighed. "That girl wasn't a skilled enough actress to pull off the guileless act. So, she MAY not know what she's messing with. On the other hand, she's half-fae. She should know better than to mess with relics. Especially relics of that sort."

We got to the lobby before I had a chance to ask her what she meant by that. Mister Wazelski waved to us. In the corner of the entryway, out of his sight, Roe stopped, a look of concentration on her face. Her form went fuzzy around the edges. If I hadn't been looking at her right then, she would have disappeared from my sight, but once again, since I was aware of the glamour, it meant I could see her. Anyone else, though, would only see a slip of a shadow, or maybe a flicker in the corner of their eye—if they were lucky.

Roe slipped out of the door, and I followed quickly after. We weren't far behind Gladys, and I spotted her walking quickly down the sidewalk. Roe hurried after her, easily slipping in and out of the crowd, and I followed after a moment, trying to keep both of them in sight.

Gladys threw a glance over her shoulder, and I ducked my head down, tugging my hat over my face a little. Not for the first time, I wished I could glamour my face. As a half-fae, the best I could produce was a thin shielding over my body that could slightly deflect a punch or a blade. When I glanced up again, I just caught sight of Roe disappearing around a corner.

Gladys led us past the business district our office was in,
through a section of town that gradually got poorer and
poorer. Tenement housing for factory workers rose up around
us, and the crowds on the street got thinner. Most folks
would be at work of the day, though there were a few men
loitering in small groups on corners who leered after Gladys.
On every block, a gang of boys—and a few girls—were
playing rowdy games of baseball in the street. As we passed
one such group, a few boys noticed Gladys and shouted after
her about Nick.

So, he was real, and not just some made-up kid. And he
really was connected to her. That was good to know.

Gladys stepped into the doorway of a building. Roe
glanced back at me, and I gave a cautious nod before walking
on, past the house, to the corner of the street. There, I stopped
and fished into my pocket for the packet of cigarettes that I
always kept there. I rarely smoked, but sometimes it was nice
to have the illusion of it as an excuse for lingering
somewhere. It didn't take long before Roe brushed against
my elbow, her silent signal that she was ready to move on.

We circled back towards our office, Roe ducking into an
alley so she could drop her glamour without startling anyone.

"You see anything?" I asked quietly.

"Hardly," Roe muttered. "She took the earrings off as
soon as she got inside the building, though. And she went

into the fourth apartment on the first floor—a guy opened the door for her, and she was handing him the earrings as she was walking in."

It wasn't much to go on. I fished my notebook from my pocket and flicked to the notes I'd been taking while Gladys talked. "It's not even her building."

"So...a reasonable conclusion would be she doesn't own the earrings," Roe said. "And she's returning them to whoever does own them."

I nodded. It wasn't a concrete fact, but it seemed reasonable.

Roe glanced up at the sky, then made a face and checked her watch. "I'll have to scoot after lunch today, Owan— sorry. I'm supposed to be at the Museum today at three for training."

I knew little enough about the Museum, except that it was located somewhere in Brooklyn and was the headquarters for the curators in New York. "No worries. I'll finish up some paperwork, maybe poke around and see if Gladys really filed a report about her missing brother."

Roe gave me a sideways look, one eyebrow raised. "I'm not going to have to rescue you again, am I?"

I chuckled. "Nope. Once was enough for me."

Roe shook her head, the motion making her curly red hair bounce around her shoulders.

When we got back to the office building, we were hailed from across the street. I glanced over and spotted a police vehicle, Detective O'Rourke leaning against the hood. He stood and jogged across the street to us.

"Glad I caught you two—I was just about to leave a note with your building's super and go to lunch." He touched the brim of his hat as he nodded to Roe. "Miss Gillam."

She smiled back. "What can we do for you today, Detective?"

O'Rourke casually glanced around the street for a moment, then lowered his voice. "You remember what I said earlier, about the fact that a few jewelry stores have been broken into lately? Well, my captain wants me to set up stakeouts at jewelry stores in the area. Figures that maybe we might catch whichever gang—or gangs—are operating, or at least get a peek at them. So, you two want in?" He shot me a grin. "It's good press for a private dick to be seen helpin' out us poor bluebacks."

I chuckled. "That's certainly something I'd be interested in. Roe?"

"Oh, no—I have classes, remember?" She elbowed me.

"Right. Sorry." I rubbed my ribcage. "Guess it'd be just you and me, Detective. You don't mind, do you, Roe?"

"Of course not. This way, if you get into trouble, there's someone to watch your back." Roe glanced at her watch, then flashed a smile at O'Rourke. "You two probably want to plan for this evening, I'd imagine. Don't worry about me, Owan— I'll find a quick lunch then catch a train to my classes." She patted me on the arm in farewell and left, walking at a sedate pace down the street.

I frowned. Roe hadn't seemed worried about it, but I hated that she'd have to miss the stakeout. It was a fantastic opportunity, not only for the case, but for her to learn more of the business. Couldn't be helped, though—curator training took precedence, on the few occasions it clashed with our work.

O'Rourke elbowed me in the same spot Roe had hit earlier. "You've got yourself a fine dame there, Craig."

"Oh, we're—she's not—I'm—"

O'Rourke laughed uproariously and slapped my shoulder. "You don't have to cover around me, boy. C'mon—let's grab some lunch and jaw about this evening. Then you can get back to whatever you were doing, and I'll pick you up tonight."

As he promised, O'Rourke picked me up that evening just around sunset. Well, I say he picked me up, but given we didn't want to draw attention, we didn't take his car. Instead, we walked several blocks to the jewelry store we were watching that night. The owner happily let us into the back entryway and showed us to the office, separated from the storefront by a velvet curtain. The room was small, and cramped with a desk, bookshelves, a workbench, and filing cabinets, but I hadn't been expecting anything like a five-star hotel. He gave us a spare key in case we needed it, then locked up and headed home.

I slid the curtain to the side, just enough that I could see the front door, and watched the sun set over the buildings around us as I turned over the events of the day. My prodding at various police stations closest to Gladys's home address had turned up at that, yes she had indeed filed a missing persons report about her little brother, one Nicholas Connor, aged twelve. So that was on the up-and-up. But if so...what was the idea about trying to fool us with glamoured jewelry? To make herself seem older, more legitimate? The way the officers I'd spoken to had talked, it seemed like Gladys had lied about her age there, too.

I didn't blame her. Chances were, if anyone official knew she was only in her teens, as Roe had guessed, that she and her brother would have been put into an orphanage or foster care, which came at risk of being separated. Still, the question of where and how she'd gotten her hands on glamoured earrings wouldn't let my mind rest. Relics were *expensive,* and this was the second case we'd run into where someone who shouldn't be able to afford them had gotten their hands on one.

"Care for a game?" O'Rourke produced a case of well-worn cards from his pocket, tapping the edge of the deck on the worktable.

"Sure, why not?" I helped him move the worktable out at a slight angle, so we could use a corner for our game. O'Rourke turned out the overhead lights, then flicked on the table map, and I adjusted the curtain so that no light would filter into the storefront.

"You have any idea when the other robberies occurred?" I asked.

O'Rourke shuffled the cards, his fingers moving in a lightning quick pattern that told me he was very experienced. I might have to watch myself—it would be embarrassing to lose a poker game in just a few rounds to a guy I was trying to impress.

"Most of 'em, the owners discovered when they came to work the next morning. In the two we've caught in progress, it's been shortly before midnight. That doesn't necessarily indicate a pattern, though."

One of those was the one Roe and I had witnessed. I propped my chin on my hand, watching him shuffle out the cards for a moment before checking my watch. It was nine o'clock, so we had some time.

We played a few rounds of poker, though I didn't have

my mind fully on the game. I could tell by the way he paused and tilted his head toward the curtain from time to time, O'Rourke didn't either, though that didn't stop him from gaining the upper hand quickly. I had no need to tilt my head—I could hear the occasional delivery van driving past on the street, and the occasional clatter of feet as folks walked back and forth. But as we sat and played, even those sounds died away, and all was quiet until about ten minutes until midnight, when someone knocked furiously on the back door. Both of us jumped, and O'Rourke grabbed for the gun strapped to his hip.

I held up my hand, listening. From behind the thick door, I could hear someone saying, "Detective O'Rourke? Detective! There's been another break-in!"

I stood, motioning for O'Rourke to put his gun away, and crossed the room, quickly unlocking the door. A disheveled-looking flattie stood in the alley, looking slightly panicked. "Where?" I demanded.

The cop blinked hard at the sudden, though dim, light coming from the doorway. "Umm—"

"What's going on?" O'Rourke demanded, pushing past me.

The flustered cop finally recovered himself enough to answer O'Rourke's question. "There was another break-in, sir. C'mon, I've been sent to bring the two of you to the scene." He gestured to the end of the alley, and I noticed the hurriedly parked vehicle there, still running. We hurried into our seats, and the cop turned, speeding down the street.

I glanced from side to side as he drove, trying to see if I could spot anything beyond the glare of the streetlights, but the alleys and storefronts flicked by too quickly.

A couple of corners and quite a few blocks later, we pulled up outside a building surrounded by several cars. By the flashlights bobbing around, I could see that several policemen had already arrived, and that the front of the store had been smashed open. O'Rourke barely waited for our car to brake before he was out the door, hurrying to the middle of the action.

I climbed out more slowly, looking at my watch in the light of the car's headlights. Not for the first time, I thought I should trade in my older watch for one of those new glow-in-the-dark ones. It would certainly make my life a bit easier.

It was just after midnight—the trip from our stakeout had barely taken ten minutes, if that. I straightened and glanced around. This time of night, there was no crowd of gawkers to fend off, so now one was paying attention beyond the circle of cars that had all parked to illuminate the storefront with their headlights. I made a show of slowly walking toward the building, but keeping my head turned away and letting my eyes slowly readjust to the darkness.

A flicker of movement in the shadows of the alley across the street caught my attention. I turned my head, watching out of the corners of my eyes. Someone was watching the commotion.

I turned my back to the watcher and stepped backward, as if wanting to survey the scene from a distance. Behind me, I could hear the rustle of clothing, but it didn't sound like anyone was trying to run for it. I slowly sidled back and to the side, still listening.

After a moment, I sprang around the corner. The watcher gasped and startled backward, and I grabbed for him, my fist closing on a rough denim jacket. The watcher made a high-pitched yelping sound as I dragged him forward.

He was a kid. A kid standing a little shorter than my shoulder line, glaring up at me, his eyes two bright green, flaring sparks under a mop of tangled dark hair. The d'anam fueinneog in his eyes was some of the strongest I'd ever seen in a half-fae, and I quickly averted my eyes.

I recalled how Gladys had described her brother to me. This kid was tall for ten, but still… "Nick?" I said.

The kid's glare deepened. "Who wants to know?" His hands moved from his jacket pockets, his fingers clenching into fists.

I shifted, so that I was holding him more at arm's length. "Your si—"

Something wrapped around my ankle and yanked. I staggered forward, hopping on one foot to stay upright. The kid wrenched free of my grip and darted back down the alley. I looked down to see that a vine had grown out of the side of the building, wrapping itself around my ankle. I kicked free of it and ran down the alley after the kid, but by the time I rounded the corner, he was long gone.

I sighed. Well, that explained one thing about this mystery...whoever that kid was, he was a Green Man. The choice of a golem was still a strange one, but at least now, the power behind it made sense.

I had to get hold of Roe.

It didn't take me long to locate a phone booth down on the corner from the crime scene. I dialed the number of Roe's boarding-house phone first, but the landlady was cranky about being woken up and refused to even check if Roe was at home. I fished my notebook out of my pocket, flipping pages until I found where I'd scribbled down the number to the Museum that Roe had given me ages ago, in case of an emergency.

I paused, considering the number. Was this really an emergency? Roe had never indicated that she wanted to keep her work with me and her lessons at the Museum separate, but... If I was honest, I didn't necessarily want to call attention to myself. I had no reason to not trust the curators, but I had no reason to trust them either. But then I thought about the dark rings under Nick's eyes and the way he had looked painfully skinny.

I sighed, shook my head, and dialed the number. The kid needed help, and I wasn't sure how to help him. Maybe Roe would have an idea.

Once the operator connected me, the phone only rang for a few seconds before it was picked up. A deep male voice answered. "The College of Curation, Professor Bronson speaking."

I raised an eyebrow. "I'm calling for Roe Gillam."

The line crackled with silence for a moment, then Professor Bronson said cautiously, "May I ask who's calling?"

I could've kicked myself. Roe had had problems with an ex-boyfriend before—though he was dead now—but it would make sense that they would be cautious of anyone asking for her. "Sorry. It's Owan Craig."

"Ah, Mr. Craig." The voice warmed. "Roe's told me about you. Let me call her."

There was a clatter, like he'd set the phone down, and I heard muffled footsteps. Less than a minute passed before I heard Roe say, "Owan?"

"Hey doll!" I said cheerfully.

Roe sighed. "Owan, it's ten after midnight. Obviously

you're fine, but what happened to the stake-out?"

"Ah, well..." I glanced over my shoulder down the street. If it were possible, it looked even busier than it had been originally. "We staked out the wrong store. They broke into a different one. That's not exactly what I'm calling about. I saw the kid."

"Nick? You saw Nick?"

"Yeah." I explained to her how I'd noticed him watching, and the way he'd escaped from me.

"He's a green man!" Roe's voice rose in excitement. "That explains the golem! Of course—the area where Gladys and Nick live is largely Jewish. Nick probably picked up on the idea of golems from his friends and did what he could with it. But...why would he be robbing jewelry stores?"

"I don't know. That's just one of the questions I'd like to ask when I find him."

Roe was silent. I knew she was thinking the same thing I was. Finding one kid, in a city of five million people? It was like we were back to square one with this case.

"Owan..." Roe's voice was very hesitant. "I have an idea. But I don't know if either you or Bear would think it was a good idea."

"Bear?"

"Sorry—Professor Bronson. All of his students call him Bear." She chuckled. "You'll understand if you ever meet him. But I think he might help us. Would—would you be okay with that? With asking him for help?"

"Uh..." All of my misgivings from earlier flooded back. "I dunno, doll, I'd have to think..." But that was the problem. I didn't want to leave Nick out on the streets any longer than we had to. I didn't *want* to take the time to think.

"Just a sec." Roe put the phone down, and I heard her muffled voice as she said something. A deeper-toned voice answered, and she picked up the phone again. "Bear says it'd be okay if you came by the Museum to meet him, if that would help. I just have this great idea, Owan, and I bet we could not only help Nick, but get answers from Gladys, too."

I sighed. "Oh, what the heck? Sure. Give me the address." Roe sounded so confident and excited, and I liked hearing her that way. Besides, what harm could it do, really? I wasn't the type of guy who trafficked in relics or glamour, and those were the sort of people the curators were after. No one would care about a half-fae private detective just tryin' to make a living. I flipped to a blank page in my notebook and jotted down the address Roe gave me, then hung up.

I'd have to get walkin'...there wouldn't be any taxis or trains this time of night.

It took me about thirty minutes of hoofing it to get to the Brooklyn brownstone at the address Roe had given me.

Thankfully, the upside of there bein' no taxis was that I
didn't have to wait for any of the new stoplights, given the
traffic was non-existent.

I knocked at the front door and it was immediately
opened by a tall, thickset man with a beard and hair that
looked like it had started the day out neatly combed, but was
now a wild mop despite his best efforts. As Roe had
promised, I immediately understand why everyone called
him "Bear".

"Welcome, Mr. Craig." He reached out, shaking my
hand. Smile ines crinkled around his dark brown eyes that
stayed, unsurprisingly, a warm shade of brown. He was fully
human, like most curators. "I'm Barnabas Bronson—you can
call me Bear, everyone does."

"Then I insist you call me Owan." I smiled back. With a
name like Barnabas, and the resultant nicknames, it was no
wonder he preferred "Bear".

He stepped back, letting me into the tiny foyer with a
parquet flooring and coat hooks lining the walls. The interior
door was already open, with Roe standing there with a grin
on her face.

"We've got it, Owan, c'mon!"

I hung up my coat and followed her. The house was high
ceilinged and narrow. Rugs layered on the floor. To the right
I could see a little sitting room lined with bookshelves. The

books seemed to be the thing tying the entire place together—the dining room's huge table was covered in stacks of books, and I spotted the golden hair of another student or teacher peeking above the stacks. Roe took the stairs two at a time and flung open a door at the top, showing me into a large space that should have been bedrooms, but was one large open room. The walls were once again lined with bookshelves and display cases. A flutter of movement caught my eye as I walked in, and I glanced to the display case to my left. A jewelry stand stood on the lower shelf, with several bracelets hanging from it. One bracelet was carved in the shape of golden wings, and as I watched the feathers stirred, stretching out a little as if they were real bird's wings stretching before a flight.

Bear must have caught my surprised look. He chuckled and tapped the glass. The feathers fluffed a little, then settled into stillness. "We store most of our relics down in the basement, in locked cases, but we keep a few up here for the students to study. They're mostly harmless."

"What does that one do?" I asked, nodding to the feathered bracelet.

Bear opened the case and pulled the sleeve of his sweater over his hand, using it to lift the bracelet out. He offered it to me.

I glanced at Roe, then back at him. Was this a test, to see

if I'd trust him? Or was he just being friendly? I took the bracelet. As soon as my fingers closed around it, I felt my feet lift from the ground. I jerked in surprise and nearly lost my balance, but Bear caught my arm, steadying me. With him steadying me, I looked down at my feet and saw that I was hovering an inch off the ground.

"Well—that just feels wrong," I remarked, handing the bracelet back to Bear. I gently thumped back to the floor, able to balance myself. "Is that it?"

Bear chuckled as he put the bracelet away. "Yes. My guess is that it was made for some fae with delusions of grandeur."

"Thought they were too good to walk on the ground like everyone else?" I chuckled. "Bet those delusions went away right quick when they flipped head over heels for the first time."

Bear laughed, the sound loud and with a rolling quality to it that made me want to join in. "Hey Roe, I like this guy better than the last schmoe you partnered up with."

I glanced over at Roe, hoping my blush didn't show. Roe rolled her eyes as she opened up a cabinet, which told me this was an old topic between the two of them. As she reached in and retrieved something small and square, Bear handed me a pair of thin leather gloves. I tugged them on and joined Roe at the table as she set the item down.

It was a small wooden snuffbox, richly lacquered in a dark color and inlaid with ivory on the top.

"I've been thinking about the problem of trying to find Nick all day," Roe said, tapping the top of the box with one finger. "About how difficult that will be. I don't suppose you had any luck talkin' to any of your cop friends?"

I shook my head. "No one's seen the kid. One guy used to walk the beat around that neighborhood and knew Gladys and Nick by sight, so at least I got confirmation of Gladys's story."

"Well, let's hope this can help." Roe flipped the box.

The underside was also inlaid with ivory, but I could see tiny ogham markings carved into it.

"If you put something in this box, I'd be able to track you." Roe glanced over at me. "Can I borrow your watch?"

I unbuckled the strap and handed it over. Folding it up, Roe could just barely fit it into the box and snap the lid shut. She murmured a Gaelic word I wasn't familiar with, and the tunes underneath the box started glowing, lighting her fingers in golden light. The box turned in her palm, pointing toward me.

Roe stepped away from my side, circling around the other side of the table. As she moved, the box continued to rotate, always pointing towards me.

I raised an eyebrow. "So you're thinking if we get

something of Nick's and put it into the box, and hopefully it will lead us to him?"

Roe nodded. "We'll find Nick, figure out what's going on with Gladys, and stop the robberies all at once. And hopefully keep the kid out of trouble."

I glanced to Bear, who had been standing back watching Roe with a gleam of pride in his eyes. "And you're okay with us using this?"

"While normally we don't encourage the use of relics, this one had no harmful side effects and seems useful." Bear's mouth quirked up into a smile on one side. "And I've always had a soft spot for kids in trouble."

"You have no idea how much we appreciate this, Bear," Roe said, handing me back my watch. She wrapped the box up into a soft piece of cloth and packed it into her satchels of tools.

"Yeah, for sure." I peeled off the gloves he'd given me and tossed them on the table, then offered Bear my hand. "Thanks. And it's been neat seeing where Roe studies."

"She's a good student. You're welcome back anytime you need help with something, Owan."

THE next morning, as Roe and I reconvened at the office, I got a phone call from O'Rourke.

"Good mornin', Detective," I said cheerfully.

"You cut outta there mighty quick last night, Craig," O'Rourke said, sounding grumpy. "Left us to do the cleanup. I was out until three AM last night."

"Sorry," I said. "Did you find anything helpful?"

O'Rourke was, unfortunately, too savvy for that trick to work with him. "I think I should be the one asking you that question."

I glanced over at Roe. She sat at her desk, studying the underside of the snuffbox and making notes in a little leather notebook. She'd promised Bear that she'd keep notes of how the relic behaved out of the control of the Museum classroom.

I was pretty sure that didn't include seeing how a certain police detective would react to it. "We're...chasing a lead," I admitted. "But keep it quiet, okay? It's a bit touch and go. I'll bring you in on it if I can."

"Okay, but if you don't, I'm claiming a favor to be called in later, Craig."

I twitched uncomfortably at the word. Did this guy know Roe and I were fae, and was just deliberately poking all the buttons he could find? Or was he clueless? I hung up and turned to Roe. "You ready?"

She nodded, slipping the relic into a velvet bag and placing the bag carefully in her satchel. We'd already gone over the plan multiple times this morning alone. We would go to Gladys and ask her for something of Nick's to put in the snuffbox. The move might attract unwanted attention, but then again, it might not--it was a gamble. Once we tracked down Nick, hopefully we could coax him into talking to us and figure out what was going on. I wasn't too sure how we'd convince him to talk to us, but Roe seemed confident.

We didn't talk much on our walk to Gladys's apartment. I could tell Roe was excited though—from what I'd gathered, the opportunity to use a relic outside of the Museum wasn't something that happened often.

We passed the apartment building Gladys had led us to last time, walking another couple of blocks before pausing in front of an almost identical building. Ideally, we'd be catching Gladys before or after her work shift—going to find the diner she'd listed as her place of employment was a possibility, but it would be easier if she was at home. We found the apartment number she'd listed and Roe knocked on the door.

Our luck held. Gladys opened the door almost instantly. "Oh," she said, surprise flitting across her face.

Before either of us could speak, a male voice said, "Who is it, doll?"

Gladys froze, her knuckles going white as she clutched the edge of the door. Over her shoulder, I saw a guy stand up from the couch in the small living area. He scowled as he came over to the door. "Who are you guys?"

As he spoke, I felt a sharp prickle wash over my skin, followed by the uneasy sense that I needed to leave. I found myself taking a step back before Roe caught my arm, halting me in my tracks. She glanced from me back to the guy standing in the doorway, and as I followed her gaze, I understood. He was fae. And as I watched, the man's face shifted slightly, revealing the pointed ears and sharper cheekbones and eyes that swirled wildly through shades of dark brown.

And he was actively using his glamour to try to drive us away.

Gladys half-turned. "It's the detectives I told you about, Angus. The ones I hired to find Nick."

The feeling of sharp unease and ill will cut off abruptly. Roe made a small noise of disdain. Whoever this guy was, he definitely didn't care about being subtle, unlike most fae.

Angus smiled at me, oozing fake gratitude. "Are you now? It's good to meet you—I'm Angus. Gladys's boyfriend."

No last name. Interesting. I shook the hand he offered to me, flaring my glamour to form a protective skin over my hand first as a precaution, and using it as an excuse to get a little too close to him. Angus's eyes flickered—he'd noticed the glamour, though he didn't say anything about it—and backed off, letting Gladys open the door enough to allow us into the apartment.

The apartment was a little larger than mine, with two doors leading off to what I assumed were bedrooms, and furnished with a couch, chairs, and shelves that looked well built, but shabby, as if they'd seen many years of use. The entire place had a slight air of disarray—a blouse flung over the back of a chair, dust on the shelves, dirty dishes in the sink—but given her work and the fact that she was missing her brother, I didn't blame Gladys for having an untidy space.

Angus shut the door behind us and grinned. "Let's just go ahead and call attention to the elephant in the room," he said. "Didn't know we had any detectives around here who were fae. Where'd you find these two, doll?"

Gladys crossed her arms, shooting him an annoyed look. "We agreed that I had to find Nick," she said. "These two have a reputation. Besides, would you rather someone else find out..." She trailed off at a scowl from Angus.

"That your brother's a green man?" Roe cut in. "That would've been nice to know at the start, Gladys."

Gladys glanced at the floor, but not before I caught her giving a quick, sideways look to Angus. The full fae held a lot of tension in his shoulders, and his smile was strained. I frowned, trying to figure out the strange tension between them. If they were a couple, they'd probably been fighting right before we showed up—though the energy between them didn't even quite match that.

"If we're clearing the air, then I have a couple of questions to ask you, Angus," Roe said. "Starting with, why did you give Gladys glamoured jewelry when she came to see us?"

Gladys flushed a little. "You saw that?" she asked.

Roe gave her a sympathetic smile.

Angus forced a grin. "Well, I mean—it ain't too different from wearing makeup to make yourself look more attractive, ain't it?" He glanced at me. "Right? We men like seein' women gussied up."

I felt my ears going slightly red.

"I'd say it's a far cry from a bit of powder and lipstick," Roe said flatly. "Relics are dangerous, not to mention—"

Angus rolled his eyes. "Spare me. You sound like a curator."

Roe's lips flattened into a thin line.

Right, well... this wasn't getting us anywhere. I stepped forward. "Angus, we came here to speak to our client." I gestured to Gladys. "I'd appreciate it if we could actually do so, rather than stand here answering tangential questions."

"I ain't stoppin' you," Angus said sourly.

"He means in private, dummy," Gladys snapped at him.

Angus's eyes narrowed suspiciously. "They might try to take advantage of a sweet kid like you, Gladys. I don't—"

"Oh, for pete's sake, get out before I throw you out myself," Roe said sharply.

At the same moment, I felt the prickle of glamour wash through the apartment. I glanced over at Roe. Her blue eyes had taken on a bright tinge, and I could see blue sparks drifting into the air from between her fingers. Angus flared his own glamour, a bright neon yellow that coiled like springs around his arms. I braced myself to jump into a fight—Roe could hold her own when it came to glamour, but I didn't like the odds of her stopping a guy near on a foot taller than her.

But I needn't have worried. Angus was a bully, and like all bullies, he didn't like being confronted by someone. The instant Roe took a step toward him, he scurried out the door, flinging one tracer of glamour that Roe deflected into the wall. I darted after him, but despite his height he was quick— he was already clattering down the stairs by the time I cleared the door.

I stepped back into the apartment, locking the door, and glanced over at Gladys. She stood by the couch, mouth slightly agape as she stared at Roe. Roe had released her glamour and was attempting to smooth her hair back down. It had somehow gotten even curlier.

"I'm sorry," she said, glancing at me. "Don't apologize!" Gladys blurted out, then turned a bright red. "I'm so sorry. I shouldn't—but, I mean... that was amazing, Miss Gillam!"

Roe glanced at the floor, looking a little embarrassed by Gladys's praise.

"So, I take it that guy wasn't your boyfriend?" I asked Gladys.

"He sure wasn't, Mr. Craig. He had some kinda nerve claimin' that, too."

I gave her a stern look. "I think it's time we get the full truth, Gladys."

Gladys looked a little scared and startled, but she nodded anyway.

"First off, why didn't you tell us your brother was a Green Man?" I asked, trying to keep the exasperation out of my voice. "He or his tree golem have been seen twice at the scene of two jewelry store break-ins."

I didn't know for certain that it had been Nick's golem at the store, but I knew I'd struck gold when Gladys's face paled. She covered her mouth with her hand. "Oh no. I'd hoped... oh, no, no, no, Nick, what are you doing?" She leaned against the back of the couch, shaking her head.

I exchanged a look with Roe.

Roe stepped forward, putting her arm around Gladys's shoulders. "Can you please explain to us what's going on?

We want to help you find your brother, but we need to know everything."

Gladys sighed, rubbing her cheeks with her fingers until they were pink from friction. "I—I'm younger than I told you guys—I'm seventeen now. I was fifteen when mom and dad died. I didn't want them to take Nick...we were all each other had...so I started pretending I was older. I found a couple of jobs that didn't poke too closely at my age. Nick was ten when they died, and... I don't know if the trauma brought out some hidden talent or somethin', but since then he's been able to do things. Help plants grow. More'n that... he can make flowers dance and bloom in the middle of winter. I knew there was the possibility that we had some kind of glamour—Mom was fae and she made no secret of it to us. She always used to joke about her magic green thumb."

Gladys laughed, though it sounded more like she was choking. "Nick got cocky with it. And last year about this time, we were..." She took a deep shuddering breath. "Angus and his gang approached us. They're all fae or half-fae, about a dozen of 'em, and they told me that Nick's talents could be put to good use. We didn't have much choice, because Angus threatened to go to the police and tell 'em I wasn't old enough to be takin' care of Nick on my own. He told me that we'd be put in an orphanage, that Nick would be adopted out..." Her voice dropped low. "I couldn't handle that."

"So... Nick began helping with robberies," I guessed.

Gladys nodded. "Just small stuff at first. Trippin' up cops by making the grass snag their ankles if they were chasin' someone, that kind of thing. But he kept pushin' Nick more and more...and then several months ago, he took Nick out in the evening and didn't bring him back until almost breakfast. Angus was happy, happier'n I'd ever seen him, and Nick looked completely exhausted. When I asked him what had happened, Nick told me that they'd broke into a jewelry store, that Angus found out he could animate a tree. That was the first I'd heard of it, too. He was so tired, Mr. Craig..." Gladys brushed tears off her face with the heels of her hands. "Angus made him go with 'em two nights later. I could tell Nick was still exhausted, so I tried to tell him they should wait, but Angus said they had a good thing goin', and it wasn't like a little exhaustion would kill the kid."

Roe pulled in a sharp breath. I glanced over at her. She pressed her lips into a thin line, shaking her head gently at me.

I admittedly knew little about glamour—enough that I could control my own. But given glamour was powered by the user's imagination and will, I could guess at the kind of effects pushing someone to use powerful glamour without enough rest could cause.

"So—Nick ran away," Roe guessed.

Gladys nodded. "I was doin' a poor job of protectin' the kid, so I guess he thought he had to take matters into his own hands." She sighed. "Angus has been on my case for weeks to find him. I've been racking my brains tryin' to think up a way to find Nick without Angus knowing."

"So you came to us," I said.

Gladys shook her head. "You were just the next people on the list. A friend who knew Nick was missing passed on your information. I didn't know, not until I got there, that you would... would understand." She sighed. "I've messed this up royally, haven't I?"

"Maybe not," Roe said quietly. She patted Gladys's shoulders. "We still might find Nick and keep him safe from Angus's crew. We'll need your help, though."

As Roe spoke, I opened the door again and stepped out into the hallway. It was clear, with all other doors still shut. I walked up to the railing of the staircase and leaned over it, looking both up and down, but couldn't catch sight of anyone who looked like they might be loitering. Irritation sawed at my nerves—not at Gladys, but at the stupid fae who thought their glamour was an excuse to do whatever they wanted. Angus and his crew didn't even sound as clever as Niall Byrnes—something that both frustrated me, and made me glad. I went to the window at the end of the hallway and looked out on the street. If I turned to my right and pressed against the glass, I could just see three men clustered at the corner of the street. Angus. The other two didn't have the sharp look of full-fae about them, but Gladys had said everyone in the gang was half-fae at the very least.

I pulled back before they could notice me and went back into the apartment. Gladys and Roe stood at the table now, with Gladys sorting through a little leather bag, talking nervously as she did so. "Some of these were Dad's, too, so they were precious to Nick." She pulled out a handful of glass marbles and picked through them, then offered one to Roe, green and gold swirls glinting in the clear glass sphere. "This one."

"That should do." Roe took the marble, tucking it into a pocket of her satchel.

"We have a problem," I told them. "Angus and two of his goons are still outside."

"Are you worried about being followed?" Gladys asked.

"That, we could handle. I'm worried about what would happen if we weren't followed," I said grimly.

Gladys, to her credit, seemed to hold up well in a crisis. She drew herself up, her shoulders squaring. "I can leave my apartment. There's a neighbor down the hall who used to watch Nick and me when we were younger, Mrs. Daniels. She'd let me stay with her, and Angus doesn't know about her."

I nodded. "That'll work. You'll have to move after this, you know that, right?"

"I've been planning on it," Gladys said quietly. "As soon as I figured out what to do about Angus."

I grinned. "Well, I can name at least one detective who would be glad to know about these guys, no questions asked." Or none that Gladys needed to worry about, anyway.

We waited until Gladys had gone down the hall and had her knock at a door answered by an old woman who still seemed hale and hearty. As she stepped into the apartment, Roe and I headed downstairs. Roe fussed with the snuffbox in her hand, checking it over several times before finally opening it and dropping the marble inside. As soon as she closed the lid, the ogham around the relic flared with a soft blue light. It tugged her hand gently to the right, and Roe closed her hand tightly around it.

As we left the building, I glanced over at the street corner. Angus and the other two still stood there. I made eye contact, made sure Angus realized that I knew what he was up to. Then I grinned at him as I turned my back and jogged after Roe. After a few moments, she glanced over her shoulder, then sighed and shook her head.

"They're tailing us," she murmured, slipping her arm around mine.

"Good," I said. "Let 'em."

It took some time and back-tracking, but eventually the snuffbox led us to a city park. By this time, it was dark, and the concession stands and neon lights of rides sent eerie, flickering lights over the shadows of the trees. We stayed on the outskirts of the park, searching through the shadows as the snuffbox rattled, moving us constantly forward.

Angus's goons still followed us at a distance, making my shoulders itch. The one good thing was that they hadn't figured out exactly WHAT we were doing—otherwise, I knew they would've tried to steal away the snuffbox.

"There." Roe tapped my arm, nodding her head at a clump of trees. Green and yellow lights from a nearby ride played over the plants, creating strange shadows. I frowned. The lights around the trees didn't quite match up to the pattern of lights from the ride.

I stepped forward, into the shadow of the trees, and felt the world around me shift. The lights grew fuzzy and pulsed in a dizzying pattern. I staggered a bit, feeling Roe caught my arm for support, and braced my hand against the trunk of a tree.

That feeling—the rough bark and cool lichen beneath my fingers—snapped my vision back into alignment. I blinked, glancing around the small clearing we now stood in. It was eerily quiet, with the faintest sound of laughter from the park, far removed from where we now stood, and muffled, as if I'd been dropped into deep water. The woods were thick around us now, the vibrant greens of the leaves and purples of the shadows almost bright enough to hurt my eyes. Fuzzy lights the size of my fist danced overhead, just out of arm's reach, the soft yellows and pinks painting the leaf-scattered ground in dappled color.

I turned and saw a rip in reality hovering in the air behind us, looking out into a copse of trees that looked much, much different than where we stood now.

"What the hell?" I whispered.

"I'm quite certain it's NOT hell," Roe answered, a faint grin tugging one corner of her lips. She untangled her fingers from mine—when had she grabbed my hand?—and stepped forward into the clearing.

The trees overhead creaked and crackled, leaves showering us. "Roe, hold up!" I darted forward.

Thick branches slammed into the ground around us, sending Roe staggering back into me. A cage of leaves and branches tightened, digging into my back. I wrapped one arm around Roe's shoulders, pulling her against my chest as I grabbed at a branch with my free hand, trying to keep it from pressing into my side. "What's going on?" I demanded.

"I don't know!" Roe grabbed at the branches in front of her, fingertips flaring with blue sparks.

A yelp sounded from somewhere in the clearing ahead of us. "Stoppit!" The voice started out as a tenor, but somewhere in the word it cracked, soaring upward in pitch as the owner yelped again. "Do that again and I'll crush you, I swear I will!"

The branches pressed tighter against us.

"Nick?" I called. "Nick, we're not here to hurt you! Gladys sent us to find you."

"Yeah right," the kid said, anger and bitterness lacing his voice. "Angus did, more like."

"We're telling the truth, Nick." Roe fumbled in her pocket, pulling out the snuffbox. It nearly wrenched itself out of her grip. She fumbled the lid open, dumping the marble into her hand, then thrust her fist through the squeezing mass of leaves and branches. "Look! She gave us one of your marbles. So we could find you."

A branch pressed into her shoulder, pushing her shoulder blade into my rib cage. I gritted my teeth to hold back a hiss of pain and heard Roe's sharp intake of breath. At any other time, gettin' this close to Roe would've been something I'd dream about, but under the circumstances...

The branches suddenly eased their hold, withdrawing back with a rustle of leaves and the groan of wood stretched beyond its limits. I took a step back, drawing in a deep, racking breath now that Roe's shoulder blade was no longer trying to replace one of my lungs. I kept my arm around her shoulders, though, and Roe didn't pull away.

The same scraggly, dark-haired kid I'd seen last night stood in front of us, holding the marble in one hand and glaring at us with eyes that shifted between the colors of the dark green forest around us. He shoved the marble into his pocket, his movements stiff and wary. "You said Gladys sent ya." He said it shortly, his face screwed into a disbelieving scowl.

"Yes." I coughed again. "Lugh's spear, kid. We're just tryin' to help."

"I wouldn't have crushed you. Not to death, anyway."

Nick crossed his arms over his chest. "I suppose Gladys wants me to come home. Well, you tell her I ain't gonna, not while Angus is prowlin' around."

My sympathy for this kid was in pretty short supply after him nearly killin' us. "It ain't your sister's fault."

"Never said it was. But I still ain't goin' home while he's loose."

Roe gently freed herself from my grasp and stepped forward. Nick flinched, but let her get near enough to put a hand on his arm. She didn't have to crouch much to get on his eye level. "Nick, we're workin' with your sister to make sure Angus won't hurt either of you anymore."

The corner of Nick's mouth twitched. "It won't matter,

not unless he and his gang is put away. And there ain't no way for that to happen without me gettin' arrested as well."

"What if we could arrange it so you wouldn't get arrested?"

I left Roe to it, tryin' to coax Nick to listen as I walked the perimeter of the clearing. The woods faded to darkness pretty quickly outside of the clearing. I didn't dare set foot out of the perfect circle formed by Nick's magic—I had no idea where we were, and I had no desire to be forever lost and wandering a dark wood like some fool in a fairytale.

I got back to the side of the clearing with the rift and glanced out, only to startle back as I realized I could see three dark figures uncomfortably close to the rift. I unbuttoned my coat, reaching for my pistol.

The figures moved slowly, and as I watched, I realized that everything outside our little bubble was moving much slower. Somehow, Nick's magic had gained us time as well as giving him sanctuary.

"Roe, we got guys incoming," I said, back-pedaling towards her and Nick.

Nick's eyes flashed a brighter green. "You led them to me!" He tried to wrench free of Roe's grip.

She dug her fingers into his shirt. "Calm down!" She snapped, and by some miracle, the sharpness in her voice made Nick go still. "This is where you can help us, Nick.

Will they be able to get in here?"

Nick nodded, a convulsive jerk of his head. "Can't figure out how to keep people out just yet."

"Okay. Well, as soon as they get inside, we'll hit them with everything we've got." I glanced at Roe. "I'll go for Angus first, but odds are you're the one who will have to deal with him."

Roe nodded grimly.

I glanced over at the rift again and saw that a hand had emerged into the clearing. And once that happened, things sped up.

Angus and his two goons stepped into the clearing. Angus's eyes locked on me and he lunged forward, the coils of glamour tightening around his arms. Before he could get within arm's reach of me, Roe hit him with a wall of her own glamour, spinning him off to the side. I ducked past him and made a beeline for one of the goons. He took a wild swing at me. I blocked it with my arm, closing in so I could get a good punch at him. As we scrapped, I noticed flashes of yellow and blue glamour out of the corner of my eye, but couldn't turn my head for fear of gettin' clobbered.

My opponent was suddenly snatched away, a branch lifting him off his feet and tossing him against the trunk of a tree.

I looked over my shoulder.

Nick huddled behind Roe, his eyes blazing a furious green and his hands upraised as he manipulated the branches of the trees to keep the two goons occupied. Roe and Angus continued to trade shots of glamour, though to my eye all it looked like was a chaotic web of yellow and blue. I ran forward and grabbed Angus, wrapping my arms around his chest and yanking him off his feet.

Roe dashed forward, one hand balled into a fist, and slammed her knuckles into his chest. Angus howled in pain and then went limp.

I lowered him to the ground and glanced around. The other two goons sprawled on the ground not far away, both out cold, probably thanks to Nick. I straightened up and glanced at him and Roe. "Okay. Let's say we get outta here."

Roe and I worked together to drag the three gangsters out of the rift and into the copse of trees by the park. Thankfully, because of the flashing lights and the excited shouts and shrieks from the rides, no one seemed to have noticed our fight.

I could go into the park and cajole one of the workers there to let me use the phone in the office to call the cops. O'Rourke arrived in record time, and to my surprise, another familiar figure followed him out of the patrol car.

"Sis!" Nick shouted, darting forward. Despite his earlier bravado, he looked on the verge of tears as he threw his arms around Gladys. She hugged him back, burying her face in his hair and rocking him back and forth.

"Well, well, this is a nice little reunion," O'Rourke commented, stepping forward. "You said somethin' on the phone about culprits in custody, Craig?"

I jerked my thumb over my shoulder at the copse of trees. "They're back there, out cold. May have a few bruises."

"I'll be sure they get checked out." O'Rourke nodded, and several constables swept past us, heading for the trees. O'Rourke, however, glanced between Roe and me, one eyebrow up. "So." He lowered his voice. "Do you have an official version of the story for me, or are you gonna leave that to me?"

I glanced at Roe. She cocked her head to the side.

O'Rourke sighed and lowered his voice even further. "My gran had the second sight, and I'm fairly certain I inherited it. That, or I've been hitting the bottle hard enough to give Miss Gillam pointed ears and make me forget I've even been drinkin'."

Roe chuckled.

I grinned and glanced over my shoulder at Nick and Gladys. They were sitting on the runner of the patrol car now, though Nick was still clinging to his sister as they talked. "Sure, I think we can sure. But let's make sure these two get back to safety first, okay?"

Thank you for reading *The Case Files of Owan Craig: Volume 1*! If you'd like to check out more of my writing, please visit www.hatitus.wordpress.com and sign up for my newsletter. You'll receive a free short story, *Stealing From the Wolves*, and an invitation to my Discord server (where you'll find a fun community of fans, receive news of sales and discounts, and have fun opportunities to get involved, like beta reading and ARC copies!)

Did you know I have an early access subscription? If you want to read my stories before anyone else, visit reamstories.com/hatitus for more info!

Acknowledgements:

Thank you to my family for the patience with my weird working hours, the ups and downs of a writer's temperament, and the times I've gone out in public with ink on my fingers and face. Love you guys so much!

Extra thanks to the members of the Edge Minecraft server. I've had much fun building things and creating stories with you, and it's been a joy to have another place as a creative outlet.

And extra, extra thanks to my beta readers who read *The Green Man* on a tight schedule and gave me such excellent feedback!

Other books by H. A. Titus:

for more fantasy and science fiction novels, visit

fayettepress.com